SCARLETT

THE SETTLERS BOOK THREE

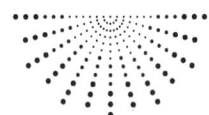

KATHLEEN BALL

Copyright © 2018 by Kathleen Ball

All rights reserved.

No part of this book may be reproduced in any form or by any electronic or mechanical means, including information storage and retrieval systems, without written permission from the author, except for the use of brief quotations in a book review.

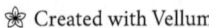 Created with Vellum

This book is dedicated to my Father-in-law Charlie Ball. He was a warm, kind, intelligent man and he is greatly missed.
Thank you to Alisa Dupre Riche for telling the story of how her parents met in Silver Falls, Oregon. It's the perfect setting for this book.
Thank you to Darren Stalk for suggesting I write about a blacksmith. Darren is a talented modern day smith who handcrafts the most incredible items.
And of course I dedicate this book to Bruce, Steven, Colt, Clara, Emery and Mavis because I love them.

CHAPTER ONE

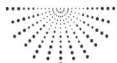

Her long, white veil whipped around her face as a gust of wind hit. Impatience was getting the better of her. She was silent as she sat next to her pa on the buckboard. A few more minutes went by, and a funny feeling hit her. Something was wrong.

When they'd arrived, her ma had hurried out of the church to tell her that Dexter hadn't shown up yet. Scarlett had nodded her understanding, confident Dexter would be there any minute. Almost a half hour had gone by, though. Where was he?

Her confidence waned as each minute passed. Her brother Hunter came out, mounted his horse and rode toward Dexter's home. It was the nicest and biggest one in town. From the minute she'd heard of the rich bachelor, she'd made it her mission to marry him. Now she was so close to her dream.

"Darlin', we have to start thinking of the possibility that he might not show," her pa said gently. He took her hand in his and held it.

Her stomach clenched. "He has to show, Pa. I'll be the

laughing stock of the whole community if he doesn't. Everyone knows I'm going to live in the big house and have the finest of everything, including servants." That couldn't happen. She'd never live it down. People would laugh at her, and she couldn't have that.

The wind blew harder, and she had a difficult time controlling her lace veil. Staring in the direction Dexter would have come, her heart sank. Finally, Hunter appeared and rode up to them, and the outraged scowl on his face said it all.

"His housekeeper told me he left on an extended trip last night. Scarlett, I'm sorry. She said he decided that marriage wasn't for him."

The pity on Hunter's face enraged her. It was the same look she was bound to get all day, and then the whispers and sneers would start. How could Dexter have humiliated her in such a fashion?

"Pa?" her voice trembled.

"Hunter, take the buckboard and get your sister home. I'll ride your horse back. I have an announcement to make." He leaned over, gently drew Scarlett into his arms, and kissed her cheek. "He shouldn't have acted the coward leaving you to face everyone. Go on home. I'll take care of it."

A chill entered her when he let her go. She watched him go into the church and then pressed Hunter to take her home. This had to be the worst moment of her life. Jilted at the altar, that only happened to ugly girls. Smoothing out her dress she regretted the money she insisted her parents spend on it. In the end it had been their wedding gift to her.

Why hadn't Dexter told her he was leaving? He could have saved her some embarrassment. They could have faced the town together and told them they weren't ready yet.

"I'm so sorry, Scarlett. Next time I see him I'm going to

blacken his eyes. It was a cruel, low down thing to do," Hunter said, his voice filled with sympathy.

Perhaps she could count on sympathy instead of being the object of vicious taunts and gossip. She highly doubted it, though. How was she to live in this town after this day? She'd so wanted to live in the big house. She'd even gone as far as to tell certain girls that had slighted her in the past, they wouldn't be invited to her teas and parties.

"Maybe Pa will give me a piece of land and build me a grand house."

Hunter frowned. "Did you even love Dexter?"

She didn't answer. Of course she didn't love him, but he was rich.

CHAPTER TWO

Three Months Later

Scarlett held a handkerchief over her nose and mouth. The dust from the stage coach was outlandish. She was stuck in the middle of the seat between two busybodies who insisted on keeping the window shades open. Across from her were three men. Two of them a bit young and excited about something, and a third who kept staring at her. He'd said they'd be there in an hour.

She was nervous about getting to Silver Springs, Oregon. It was a newer town, and she hoped she would find it had all the conveniences she was used to. Water pumped into the house, a cook stove, and a dress shop. She couldn't wait to meet the other women at teas and become part of the planning committee for founders' day and other holidays. She'd have a brand new start…and a husband.

She hadn't had much luck getting anyone to court her, so she'd decided to widen her search and found the most respected man in Silver Springs, Dillon Stahl. She loved his name. She'd always pitied mail order brides before, but now she realized there was no shame in being one. In fact it took courage to marry a man she'd never met.

Of course they'd exchanged a few letters, and her pa knew him from his travels guiding Pioneers to Oregon. Her pa said Dillon was a good man. He owned the biggest establishment in town, and he went to church. She had only skimmed the letters. He was a man of means and respect, and that was all that mattered.

The coach slowed, and excitement began to course through her. She was finally going to get what she wanted. Amid more choking dust, the coach came to a stop, and the other passengers all fought to get out first. She sat and waited. There was no way she wanted to be near the sweaty men, and perhaps some of the dust would settle.

Then it was time. Chin up and shoulders squared, she placed a foot onto the step the coach driver had put in place. She steadied herself by taking his hand and nodded her thanks as she finished disembarking. Then she stood on a wooden walkway and scanned the town. There really wasn't much to see. They had stopped in front of the general store and she studied each man, but none seemed to be her Dillon.

The coach driver lifted down her three trunks and set them on the walkway. "Where would you like these, miss?"

"I'm waiting for my groom. Just leave them right there."

He nodded and stepped back. "Have a good day." He tipped his hat and climbed back onto the driver's seat. More dust mixed with mud rose as the stagecoach pulled away, and Scarlett wrinkled her nose, trying not to cough.

As the dust settled again, she took a deep breath, stood straight and tall, and held her head high, the way she imagined a princess might carry herself, or at least a lady of fine breeding. The only man still standing in front of the store was a man covered in black dust wearing a leather apron.

She immediately discounted him and continued to watch for her groom.

"Miss Settler?" the dust-covered man asked.

"Yes, that is me."

"I'm Dillon Stahl. I'm mighty glad to meet you. I'm sure the trip was long, but I have one more thing I need to take care of before I can call it a day. We'll just leave your trunks here, and you can come to my shop with me."

She widened her eyes. This couldn't be the most respected man in town with the biggest establishment. He had a headful of blond hair and his blue eyes appeared kind, but still. "If you could just direct me to the hotel, I'll be fine."

"Silver Springs doesn't have a hotel yet. Come, it won't take long, Miss Settler. May I call you Scarlett?" His smile was nice enough.

She wanted to say no, but good manners prevailed. "Of course you may call me Scarlett." She'd find a way out of this before nightfall.

"We'll leave your trunks here. No one will bother them. I'd offer you my arm but as you can see I'm covered in soot. We don't have far to go, just across the street."

She turned her head and there was the blacksmith shop. It was big. Bigger than any she'd seen before. Did he live there too?

Dillon stepped off the wooden planks and into the street of mud. He turned and held out his hand for her.

Scarlett wrinkled her nose at the mud and then lifted her skirt just enough to reveal her dainty shoes. They wouldn't make it across.

"Is there somewhere dryer I could cross?"

Dillon shook his head and stepped back on the walkway. He opened the door to the Store and went in. A moment later, he came back out carrying a blanket. "I'll carry you across using this blanket so I don't get your pretty dress dirty."

She nodded, finding herself at a loss for words, which was unusual for her. She waited for Dillon to step back into the mud. Then she wrapped the blanket around her body and held herself rigid as he lifted her into his arms.

He laughed. "Relax, love. You're as stiff as a poker. Wrap your arms around my neck. I won't bite."

She did as he asked, and she could feel just how powerful his arms were. His shoulders were broad and his chest seemed well muscled. Not at all like Dexter. Disappointment hit her when he set her down, and she mentally berated herself. She had decided long ago not to love. Everyone she loved died, and she couldn't handle it if another person was called home by God.

Dillon took her hand and led her inside the building. "This is my smithy. I have two apprentices, who I told to take the rest of the day off. But at the last minute one of the farmers needed a wheel fixed, and I promised to get right to it."

He walked her to a stool and had her sit down. "You should be safe here."

Safe? What in the world?

She watched as he worked the bellows getting the fire hotter. It was more than sweltering inside the shop, uncomfortably so.

"I thought wheels were made of wood," she commented.

"Not the wheel rim. I try to repair when I can to save my customers money, but this old rim has been repaired beyond its usefulness."

She watched as he placed metal in the coals, waited a bit and then started pounding it with a hammer. He did it again and again. Every once in a while he'd have to work the bellows to make the fire hotter. Then he'd put the metal in, take it out and pound on it. Finally he placed it around the wagon wheel and smiled.

"A great fit. Sometimes they can be a bit tricky, depending where they got the wooden wheel from. I'll finish up in a minute."

"I'm feeling a bit woozy from the heat and that black stuff. I'll be outside."

He nodded as he continued to fit the rim to the wheel.

She stood on the boardwalk breathing in the fresh air. What was she supposed to do? She spied two women walking her way and put a bright smile on her face.

"You must be, Scarlett," The older one with white hair said. She was well dressed, and immediately Scarlett wanted her for a friend.

"Yes, I am. I just arrived today. Tell me, is there a boarding house or do you know of anyone with an extra room?"

"Whatever for?" The other woman about the same age as Scarlett asked, frowning.

"I'll need a place to stay."

"Oh where are my manners? I'm Olga Gloss and this is my daughter Elda. Don't mind Elda, she's a bit upset that Dillon is getting married. They'd been friends for a long time. Scarlett, dear, it was told to me that you'd be wed this evening. You won't need a place, not that there's any room. Most of the families are living in their covered wagons or in tents waiting for the saw mill to catch up so they can start building. It's so exciting to see our little town grow. Why they're putting a post office on this street soon."

"I'm getting married tonight?"

"Yes. Didn't Dillon tell you? We do have a church up on the hill over there."

Scarlett looked to where Olga pointed. "It looks very nice."

"He'd best hurry if he plans to be soot free. You're a lucky girl. He's the best man I know. We tried to get him to be the mayor, but he declined. I'm glad he'll have someone to take care of him."

Elda laughed. "And someone to do his laundry. It's hard work getting his clothes clean."

Scarlett stared at Elda. How would she know about an unmarried man's laundry?

Olga put her hand on Scarlett's arm. "We take turns washing for him. He pays well, so it's worth the extra trouble."

"Olga, Elda! It's good to see you," Dillon said as he joined them outside.

"Dillon Stahl! I should take a switch to you. This poor gal didn't know she was getting married tonight. She was asking about a boarding house," Olga scolded.

His brows rose. "It was in my letters."

Heat rushed into Scarlett's face. "I read the earlier letters, and once you proposed I was so excited and busy packing I guess I didn't read them carefully enough."

"You do know how to read, don't you?" Elda asked.

"Graduated from school and everything, Elda." Scarlett kept a smile on her face but it wasn't easy. She glanced across the street. "Dillon, my trunks are gone."

"They must be at the house. People in this town are helpful and friendly. I'm glad. I only rode my horse this morning, not thinking about how you or your trunks would get to the house."

Olga smiled. "We'll see you two at the church." Then she grabbed Elda's hand and hurried off. Elda kept her gaze on Dillon the whole time.

"Come, love. I go out the back to get home."

Scarlett suppressed a scowl. He'd have to stop calling her love, but now wasn't the time to tell him. The town had wanted him to be mayor? What kind of town was this? She followed him, wondering how to tell him she wouldn't marry him.

He led her out the back where his horse was saddled and waiting.

"Is the house far?"

"No. Look up. It's on the second rise."

Her jaw almost dropped. It was the biggest house she'd seen this side of the Mississippi River. Nothing added up. How could this dirt-covered man be so wealthy?

"Come, I need to clean up before we head to the church."

The next thing she knew he plucked her up and put her on the horse sideways and then he hopped on behind her. It was very strange to have his arms around her again as he slowly rode to his house. Dexter had only hugged her once. She looked down at his strong hands and saw the soot on the front of her dress and frowned.

It simply wouldn't do. He'd simply have to find another profession that wasn't so dirty. She had to bite her tongue so she didn't take him to task.

The house was even bigger than it looked from the bottom of the hill. It reminded her of plantations in the South that she had once read about. Perhaps his parents lived there?

"Did you write the letters?" He sounded suspicious.

"What?" she asked.

"Did you write the letters you sent me?"

"Yes I did but I had some help. My sister Cindy thought they were too dry and boring." She turned her head, watching him.

He nodded and his lips formed a grim line.

"What?" she demanded. "What are you thinking about?"

"Cindy is probably the romantic."

"Oh, you mean looking up at the stars? Yes, she wrote

that. I enjoy it but it wouldn't occur to me to write about it. She wanted to write about love and babies but I forbade it."

"I see." He still looked grim as though he was disappointed and angry.

"I've said something wrong, haven't I?"

"No, the truth is always best. You do want children, don't you?"

She could tell from the tone of his voice that this was the question that could get her out of the marriage. She thought to tell him no but gazed into his blue eyes. He was so handsome, and he did have a big house.

"I have a lot of experience with babies and children. My parents have a houseful."

She must have said the right thing because he slowly grinned. It was a heart stopping type of grin that she'd have to grow immune to.

HE GOT off his horse and reached up for Scarlett. She sure was as light as a bird. A very small bird. "Go on in. I have to unsaddle Coal here. Before you ask, it's spelled C-O-A-L like the coal I use in my work."

"Clever." She turned and opened the door.

Dillon shook his head. He had a bad feeling about the whole marriage thing. His friend Smitty had said she was a bit high strung but Dillon was beginning to think he'd been duped. She hadn't even written the letters. Plus he'd seen the look of disdain on her face a few times.

"What do you think, Coal? Does being a man of my word mean I have to go through with the wedding?" Dillon thought on it as he unsaddled and fed the horse.

Smitty had written that she'd been jilted at the altar and she wanted to get away from the town since she was the subject of scathing gossip. Dillon owed Smitty big time. On the way from Missouri to Oregon, Smitty had pulled him from a burning wagon.

"Coal, I am a man of my word." He patted the horse's neck and left the barn. He'd built the house bigger than necessary but his plan was to fill the rooms with his children. He wanted a family.

He hurried into the house. It was going to take a bit of time to get cleaned up. Scarlett stood waiting in the hallway. He had to admit she was lovely.

"You don't have a water pump inside? What about a cook stove? Most of the rooms aren't furnished."

He took a few breaths before addressing her. "I wanted my bride to be able to make this house her own. Frankly, I've been so busy working. I haven't had time to get a cook stove, and the creek isn't far if you need water." He'd already made arrangements to get a water pump, but he didn't like her attitude or her harping.

She put her hand over her mouth then removed it. "I have a bad habit of talking before I think. It's a beautiful house, and you're right I can haul water. It's my worst flaw and my biggest. I try to watch what I say, but words just pop out, and words are hard to take back. I've been known to tell a woman her dress is ugly."

No wonder she had to leave her home. Dillon's lips twitched and then he laughed. She certainly wasn't boring, and she didn't mean to be a shrew. At least he hoped not.

"What's so funny?" She crossed her arms in front of her.

"Before you feel hurt, I was just thinking we'd make an interesting pair."

Dillon poured warm water into two basins and handed one to Scarlett. "You take the bedroom. I'm going to have to rinse out the basin a few times to get the grime off."

He waited until she closed the door and then he pulled off

his shirt. Maybe she could make him a few shirts for work. He always cut the sleeves short so as not to get burned. A spark could fire up on him. He grinned again as he washed. She must have thought he was a drifter when she first met him.

He threw the dirty water out the back door and poured more clean water into the basin. This was the only part of the job he hated, but it was just dirt. He made a great living doing something he loved. Working with his hands crafting metal was well worth the soot. He didn't think Scarlett would agree, though.

Finally, dressed in his finest black suit, he then put on his Sunday go-to-church boots and hat. The jingle of harness buckles and the clop-clop of horses' hooves came from outside, signaling the surrey being driven up out front. He opened the door and waved to one of his apprentices, Homer. He was a fifteen-year-old boy who was on his own. Dillon had built a small house for Homer and his other young apprentice Lou. They hadn't given him a lick of trouble, and he was glad he'd taken them on.

"Scarlett? The surrey is here."

"I'll be right out," came her muffled response.

He might as well sit. Women took forever getting ready. Just as his backside hit the seat, the bedroom door opened. He couldn't keep his jaw from dropping when he caught sight of Scarlett. He stood up and stared. Her beauty outshined any other woman he knew.

Smiling she turned in a circle. "Will I do?" She turned around in her fine yellow dress that cascaded from her waist down. The bottom half had a beautiful fine lace overlay.

"I'll be the envy of every person in town with you on my arm."

Obviously pleased, she beamed at him. Now he knew why people said a bride looked to be glowing. He offered her his arm and led her outside. He had to carry her to the surrey to avoid the mud. As soon as he got in, it started to rain.

"Scarlett, this is Homer, one of my apprentices.

"Nice to meet you, Homer," she said.

Homer tipped his hat but remained silent.

"Let's get going before the mud sucks us in." Dillon took her hand in his, and she shivered. "Cold?"

"No, just nervous."

"It'll be fine. This time you have your groom with you."

Scarlett's eyes flashed and her lips formed a frown. "I bet you had a good laugh at that. Am I being laughed at by the town's people?"

"No. I'm sorry. Your pa told me when he wrote to me about my intentions. I shouldn't have brought it up. I don't want to ruin our wedding."

"Fine. I forgive you." She sounded as though she was doing him a big favor. She turned her head and looked at the scenery all the way to the church.

THE CHURCH WAS LESS primitive than she'd thought it would be. It had a tall steeple with a bell. She'd never seen one like it before, though she'd heard of them. Many horses and buckboards stood waiting in the rain. There must be a lot of people inside.

Boards of wood had been laid on top of the mud so they could walk without getting stuck, but Dillon swept her up in his brawny arms and carried her. He was quick about it, and she held her cape over their heads to prevent them from getting too wet. Once inside, she hung her cape on one of the hooks along the rear wall and smoothed out her dress. It felt bittersweet to get married without her family being present.

"I'm Dinah Bains, dear. Dillon, get to the front of the

church and stand next to Terry. I'm so glad both you boys cleaned up. Now, here is your bouquet," the older woman with fading red hair said as she handed a lovely bouquet of yellow ox-eye sunflowers, light purple coneflowers and dark purple larkspur to Scarlett. "I have to go up front and play the piano. There will be some music, and then my daughter Melly will go down the aisle first. Once she gets to the front, I will play the wedding march. I'm so excited. This is the first wedding in Silver Falls that the march will be played at. You walk down the aisle and hand your maid of honor, Melly, your bouquet and then stand next to Dillon. After that, the minister will direct things."

Before Scarlett could ask any questions, Dinah scurried up front. A stunning redheaded woman who looked about Scarlett's age stepped in front of her. A white, low-cut dress showed off her assets.

Scarlett smoothed down her own yellow dress and shook her head. "Why are you wearing white, um…?"

"Melly, my name is Melly. It looks good on me. When I saw the dress I just had to have it." Melly tried to look innocent, but Scarlett didn't believe her. Everyone knew that only the bride wore white.

"Why aren't you wearing white?" Melly covered her mouth momentarily. "I'm sorry. It's none of my business. White means the bride is pure."

"Perhaps, but not this far west. It wouldn't be practical." Her white dress had been for Dexter, and she'd ripped it to pieces.

The music started, and Melly strutted down the aisle waving to everyone.

Taking a deep breath, Scarlett concentrated on Dillon at the altar. He was so handsome.

Her music started, and she gracefully walked down the aisle smiling while staring at her groom the whole time.

She'd meet the guests later. For now, she wanted to show up Melly by being appropriate and showing class. When she tried to hand her bouquet to Melly she refused to take it.

Scarlett gave her a sweet smile and then shrugged. She turned back to Dillon and smiled. She wondered if she should be praying. She was in a church. She said a quick silent prayer for a happy marriage.

It was time for Dillon to put the ring on her finger. He turned to his best man to get it and then slowly slid it onto her finger.

She stared at the ring. She'd never seen anything like it. It was made of three gold strands that looked to be braided. It was so beautiful. She lifted her face and gazed into his eyes, and from the questioning look he had, she knew he'd made it for her. She gave him a real smile, not one of her usual pretend smiles, but a real one. It'd been a long time since she had smiled that way.

He smiled back and when it was time, he gently took her into his arms, leaned down, and brushed his lips over hers. She anticipated more, but he let her go. Didn't he want to kiss her? Confused she glanced at Melly, who seemed amused.

That was it. The wedding was over. Dillon held his arm out to her and whisked her away to the surrey. He carried her again, but it didn't feel any different. He didn't hold her closer to his chest. Homer flicked the reins as soon as they were settled. She expected to be taken to a reception but Homer drove them to the house. Was the party going to be held at his home?

Homer stopped the surrey close enough to the porch steps that Dillon only needed to offer his hand to help her down. She waited to be carried over the threshold, but Dillon opened the door and yanked his tie off.

"Whew, that's done. I'm going to change out of these clothes right quick. I'll be back directly."

She didn't say a thing, just stood in the middle of the big, practically empty room with her flowers in one hand and her ring on the other. She had no idea what it all meant, but her heart hurt. Ever since she was a small child, she'd dreamed about how her wedding would be, and part of that dream included dancing with her husband and toasting to their happiness. He hadn't even introduced her to his best man.

Was he ashamed of her? Did the story of her being jilted make her just a convenient bride who didn't need more? She missed her ma and pa something fierce. Tears pricked at the back of her eyes, but she refused to cry. She'd have to make the best of it. This was her second chance, there wouldn't be another.

She put a smile on her face when Dillon came into the room. She waited for him to say something, but he remained silent. What had she done wrong?

A frantic knock on the door broke the silence, and Dillon left the room to answer it. Scarlett followed but stopped short when she saw it was Melly.

"If you don't bed her then there is still a chance for us. Just because her father saved your life doesn't mean you have to sacrifice your happiness for him." Tears streamed down Melly's face. "I wore the dress I bought for our wedding, and the whole time my heart was breaking."

Dillon sighed. "Melly, go home. I'm married, and I can't have you knocking on my door. I'll talk to you soon. Please, Melly, you need to go home."

Scarlett went into the bedroom she'd used to get dressed and locked the door. She sat on the bed and folded her hands together. Her humiliation knew no bounds. Dry eyed, she stared at the wall until she saw the light from under her door dim and become dark. He hadn't knocked on the door or talked to her. Why did he act so nice before the wedding only to be cruel afterwards?

She'd been nervous about the wedding night, but her ma had explained it to her. It certainly didn't bode well for their marriage if this was how he would be acting. What did Melly mean? Had Pa rescued Dillon? Her breath stalled in her throat. That just made her a favor, an owed favor. They'd all lied and betrayed her. What about Melly? She wore her wedding dress? How mixed up it all was.

Melly had been right about one thing; the wedding wasn't binding unless they consummated it. Given the chance, Scarlett wanted to run and hide. She'd go someplace where she wouldn't be an obligation. Dillon must feel as though he'd been hogtied and dragged to the altar. He was too nice of a person to be stuck with her. She'd go home. It would be the right thing to do.

She changed into her nightgown and smiled as she fingered the pink ribbon she had sewn on it. She'd make everything right in the morning.

CHAPTER THREE

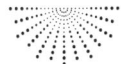

The next morning, Scarlett dressed and packed her things. She walked into the kitchen and was surprised to see Dillon sitting at the table already eating his breakfast.

"Good morning," he said as he wiped his mouth with his napkin. "Can I get you some coffee?" He acted as though nothing was wrong.

"I can get it. Thank you for making it. Do you always get up before the sun?" She poured herself a cup of coffee and sat in a chair across the table from him.

"My work is never done it seems. Someone always needs something made or repaired. And I like to have designs of my own for sale too. Then there is the occasional tooth to pull, house plans to draw. I usually work twelve to fourteen hours a day."

"Don't they have a barber to pull teeth?"

"Not in this town, at least not yet. I always have men dropping in to say hi. That's why I have those stools in there. Right now, my apprentices are cleaning out the forge and putting new coal in it. Then they make the fire hot so the coals will be hot enough to soften the metal. Then Homer will make a list of things we need to get done. Of course, people come in all day wanting things fixed immediately." He smiled at her.

"Sounds like a lot of work but you like it."

"Yes, I do like it, and I'm good at it. People know to stop here before going on to mine the gold fields. I have the best tools and at a good price. If I had the time, being Mayor would have been nice but I have a wife now so I have to have a few minutes to spare for her." A smile played at the corners of his mouth as he gazed into her eyes.

She couldn't read him. He didn't look like a man trying to be rid of her. Heat flooded her face. "I'll be on today's coach heading back home. If you could make arrangements for my trunks to be put in front of the general store, I'd appreciate it."

His fork clattered against his plate. "No."

She gave him her most haughty look. "No? I think you're mistaken. Things aren't working out for us, and I'm leaving."

He took a sip of his coffee as he stared at her. "You know we won't suit in less than twenty-four hours? I've been told I'm a catch. Let's see I haven't yelled at you or beaten you. I haven't hurled insults at you. In fact, I think I've been very accommodating toward you. No, I said my vows in a church and I refuse to break them." He cocked his left brow. "Is this because I didn't come to your bed last night?"

Warmth seeped into her cheeks to an uncomfortable level, and she quickly glanced away. This wasn't going as planned. "You married me as a favor, and your true intended wore her wedding dress to *our* wedding. I bet the whole town is laughing at me now. Why I thought being a mail order bride would be a good idea, I have no idea. I have two brothers who are married, and I see the way they look at their wives. They are in love with their wives, and I didn't understand that before, but it's what I want."

"You might grow on me," he teased with a grin.

"It's not funny. I wasn't your choice at all. I can't wait to see my pa. He'll get an earful!"

"Listen, Smitty didn't make me do anything. I do what I want. No one is laughing at you. I never courted Melly. She just got it in her head that we were meant to be." He leaned forward and pinned Scarlett in his gaze. "I'm *your* husband. And just so you know, I was showing you respect by sleeping in my own bed last night. You don't know me, and I want to wait until the right time. I want to wait until we feel something for each other. That way it will be less awkward."

She swallowed hard. It wasn't her fault that she came to the conclusions she had. "And if I never feel a thing for you?"

"Who knows? I might not feel a thing for you. I think we should give it a try anyway. Look, no one is going to believe that we didn't consummate our marriage. You're living with a man, so I'd get the idea of leaving out of your head." He sounded irritated.

She'd thought he'd be relieved to be rid of her. She could be a huge pain and thought he might just want to be rid of her. She finished her coffee and stood. "Let me grab my reticule and we can be off."

He frowned. "Off to where?"

"To work, of course. I want to know all about you and spend time with you. I'll be able to see you in action."

"Are sure? It's a long day. Do you have knitting or the like to keep you busy?"

"Actually, I do. I'm making you a scarf. Don't leave before I find it." She hurried to her room, smiling. She was already becoming a thorn in his side. She didn't believe the Melly story. Who bought a wedding dress if they hadn't had encouragement from a man?

She took her time and when she went back to the kitchen, he was gone. She hurried outside to see if she could catch him. The wagon was hitched with two beautiful gray horses. Her family was in the horse business, but she couldn't tell one from another. She waited for Dillon to carry her but he climbed up onto the wagon bench and looked at her.

"Are you coming?" There was a challenge in his eyes.

She'd show him! She lifted her skirts just enough to avoid getting her hem dirty and began to walk to the wagon. She made it more than halfway, silently bemoaning the ruining of her shoes, before she got stuck. She almost fell face first, but she was able to regain her balance. The mud was so thick it sucked at her feet, not wanting to let go. Her shoulders sagged. She'd failed his challenge.

"I need some help." He sat there for a moment while she stared at him. Finally, he jumped down, splattering mud in her direction and all over her dress.

He took her bag from her and threw it into the wagon, but instead of picking her up, he tugged her hand until she was able to raise her foot. She finally was able to walk with him pulling her along. He lifted her into the wagon and then climbed up beside her.

She tried to smooth her dress, but she only succeeded in spreading the mud. Glancing down at her shoes she was horrified to see so much mud caked on them and the hem of her dress was clumped with the horrible wet dirt.

She gave him a sidelong look and found him smiling. If this was to be a competition of wills, then Dillon wouldn't know what was about to hit him. She could be as stubborn as anyone, and she wouldn't beg for mercy. She'd think of something horrible to make him for dinner.

He drove down the hill and parked behind his shop. This time he lifted her down and set her in front of the open door. "Go on in."

She walked in and was surprised to see what had been walls yesterday were now open. They were huge sliding doors. The coals looked hot and there was only one stool left. He must be very popular to have so many men sitting waiting for him.

She nodded at the men as they stared at her, and then she sat down. Homer quickly ran over with a fresh bandanna. "Ma'am, you have mud on your face. Here, use this." He gave it to her and hurried back to working the bellows to get the coals hotter.

She clamped her mouth closed. Dillon had known she had mud on her face and hadn't told her. The bandana was soft against her skin as she wiped her face. She did the best she could, trying to get the mud off, but without a mirror she couldn't be sure she'd gotten it all. How utterly embarrassing.

At last, Dillon came in, wearing his big leather apron. He smiled at her. "Comfortable? Here's your bag." He took the bandana from her hand and finished wiping her face. Then he handed the cloth back to her. "Gentlemen, this is my wife Scarlett. She wanted to see how I work. So, in deference to her, please watch your language."

Many nodded, but there were a few grumbles. She smiled at all the men, even the grumblers. It was only good manners not to cuss in front of a lady. She took out her knitting and started. She'd decided on a natural color since she hadn't known what color coat he wore. The scarf took on length as she sat and listened. She was amazed at how gossipy the men were.

She didn't know who they were talking about, but she knew to stay away from someone named Harvey. It was rumored he had consumption. A woman named Matilda had a rash on her backside. How they knew *that*, Scarlett couldn't imagine. It went on and on. Perhaps once she got to know who they were talking about, it might be entertaining.

The stool was very hard and uncomfortable, and there were only a limited amount of positions she could use to sit on it. She shifted yet again then turned and watched Dillon. He was so confident in his work. Lou and Homer seemed to know what he needed before he had to ask, and they worked in unison. It was growing extremely warm in the shop.

Every once in a while Dillon would glance her way. Probably making sure she hadn't fallen off the hard stool. Men came and went, and she ended up hearing about Matilda's rash in greater detail, and when she figured out that Matilda was a whore, she'd about had enough but she just smiled at Dillon every time he looked at her.

The mud dried, and she got up and went onto the boardwalk, where she tried to brush the dirt from her dress. A good amount came off, but she was still a mess. She kicked her shoes against the side of the planks and much of the heavy mud dropped off.

It was nice and cool outside compared to the heat of the shop, but she supposed she would have to go back inside eventually. She reflected on her morning observing Dillon. She had seen respect in his customers' eyes. They relied on him to fix their tools. He'd shod many horses today so far, too. The work had been nonstop for him. One man needed to know how to make a chicken coop, and Dillon had taken time out of his work to patiently explain it, and then he had drawn a picture for the man. Dillon was well appreciated.

She walked the length of the boardwalk and was surprised to see a river not too far away. A turn toward the north revealed what she thought might be a waterfall among the dense trees. From what she could make out, it looked lovely. She observed a row of houses behind the buildings across the road. Farther out were parked wagon trains and tents.

And then she spotted women walking to the general

store. Most waved at her, and she felt warm inside. They too had mud on the hems of their skirts, but they seemed to have much sturdier shoes. If only she had taken her ma's advice. But she had only pictured herself at teas and parties. Oh, bother! She hadn't saved any of the money Dillon had sent her or the money her pa had given her. She bought more dresses, pretty ones. She couldn't very well ask Dillon for boots after she told him she wanted to leave, could she?

WHACK! Dillon struck the metal piece on his anvil with a heavy hammer then tensed and stared at his project. He'd almost hit his hand, and he never made mistakes like that. Where was she? Her presence was too distracting, and his job was dangerous. But not knowing where she'd gone was worse. He finished the fire grate he was making then he wiped his hands. They'd become black from the oxidation of the metal. Every work shirt and pair of trousers he owned had black spots on them. It was to be expected, and usually he paid little mind. Today, though, things seemed...different.

He was just about to step out onto the walkway to find Scarlett, but she came in before he had the chance. "Is everything all right? You were gone for a time."

She nodded. "I was looking at the river and what I think is a waterfall. It's quite pretty here. Well except for the mud."

"There are ten waterfalls in all. This is our rainy season. When things dry out a bit I'll take you to see the falls."

She didn't respond. Instead, she sat back down on her stool and got her knitting out. Dillon's jaw clenched. She probably didn't think she'd be here when the rainy season ended. Well, she could think what she wanted, but she wasn't going home. Maybe she didn't know how her name was being bandied about where she'd lived. He didn't want the same thing for her here.

There was a new group of men hanging around. He told each man who walked in to watch his language because his wife was visiting today. His lips twitched as Fred Young cussed up a storm anyway. Scarlett pretended not to hear, but she turned bright red.

"Hey have you heard about Matilda's rash? Oh boy it's covering—"

"Excuse me but I don't want to hear about poor Matilda's problem anymore. That's been the main topic of discussion in here. Have any of you sent a doctor to see her? Many of you have claimed to have seen it. Did any of you try to help her? Did anyone bring her some salve?" Scarlett looked at each man as she spoke.

They all remained silent, some shifting their gazes to the ground.

"I didn't think so."

"But ma'am," Fred said. "She's a whore."

Dillon groaned out loud.

"She's still a person you all seem to go to see. Has anyone offered her a better job? Usually it's women down on their luck that become, well they become—"

"Whores," Fred supplied. He opened his mouth to say something further, but it seemed Scarlett's withering glare stopped him.

Dillon didn't know whether to laugh or not. She was still glaring, so he decided not to. "No more talk about Matilda or any other females with problems."

"What about the new one named Candy? She sure doesn't have any problems," Fred said with a low chuckle.

"Fred, don't talk at all today," Dillon said, causing the rest to laugh.

"Sounds like you're having a good time in here," Terry

Boxer said as he took off his hat and gave Scarlett a slight bow. "You look most enchanting, Scarlett. May I call you Scarlett? I'm Terry Boxer your husband's best—and I think best-looking—friend."

Scarlett smiled sweetly. "You are quite a contrast, aren't you? Dillon with his blond hair and blue eyes, and your brown hair and eyes. But I haven't met all his friends to know if you speak the truth."

Terry laughed and turned toward Dillon. "She's perfect for you."

"You think so?" Dillon asked.

"I do think so. Too bad that storm was expected last night and everyone had to hurry home. I would have loved to celebrate your marriage. Actually, that is why I'm here. Nora and Patty decided you need to have your party this Saturday at my place."

"Well if both of them decided then there is no choice." Dillon turned to Scarlett. "Nora is his housekeeper and Patty is his daughter both wonderful but a little bossy."

Scarlett smiled. "Saturday it is. I'd—we'd be delighted to attend."

"I see Lolly is heading over with your noon meal. I'll return and tell the two conspirators that they can have their party. It was nice to meet you, Scarlett." Terry nodded his head to her before he slapped Dillon on the back.

"You all know the rules, everyone out so my men can take their break," Dillon said.

Both Homer and Lou puffed out their chests when he called them men.

Lolly came in with a great big smile that she bestowed on Dillon. He smiled back until he remembered not to.

"Lolly, this is my wife, Scarlett. Scarlett, this is my dear friend, Lolly." He watched as Lolly's smile slipped away and Scarlett's eyes glittered. "Lolly and I have been friends since forever." Scarlett's eyes then narrowed. Dang, he'd said the wrong thing. "I mean our folks were friends and we all came to Oregon together. Lolly you remember Smitty, don't you? This is his daughter."

"It's nice to meet you, Scarlett. I'll just set the food on the counter. My little one is waiting for me to come back. Lou, could you bring the dishes to me on your way home? I'm not sure I'll be able to swing by later to get them."

"Yes, ma'am."

Lolly's smile was strained. "Good bye." She turned and walked through the mud to her house.

Dillon watched after her then turned with a sigh. Usually she talked to him a bit.

"Scarlett, pull your stool up to the counter. It's the easiest way for us to eat. We can share a plate." He was surprised when she didn't say a word but carried her stool over to the counter. She sat and waited for him to join her.

"Oh boy! Fried chicken," Lou exclaimed.

Dillon sat and took Scarlett's hand. "Lolly is a good cook. Her husband died last year and she's been making money cooking for us and others. She has a daughter…" He wasn't sure what else to say. Scarlett's eyes still glittered.

"The chicken does smell good," she said.

He squeezed her hand gently and then put chicken, biscuits, and green beans on their plate. He hadn't known Lolly had a thing for him. He walked through life oblivious sometimes. The hurt on her face would haunt him for the rest of the day.

After they ate, he had Homer drive Scarlett home. She didn't object at all. He probably wouldn't have to worry about her wanting to watch him work again.

SCARLETT

AFTER SHE REACHED the front door, she turned and waved at Homer. He was a nice, young man and a good servant. She then let herself in and took off her ruined shoes. Dillon must play fast and loose with the women of Silver Falls. First Melly and now Lolly and probably Elda too. Did he even know he was breaking hearts? He didn't act as though he knew, or maybe he just didn't care.

She knew nothing about her husband, absolutely nothing. Thank goodness he wanted to wait a while before they shared a bed. Why did those women act so hurt that Dillon had married? Maybe he couldn't decide between them so he picked her.

Her back and bottom hurt from sitting on the stool. Poor Matilda and her rash. Suddenly she broke out in laughter. Men were so gossipy. She wouldn't have imagined. It put a whole new light on the words kiss and tell. She thought of the unfortunate Matilda again. She had plenty of salves for healing. Her ma was a healer. She couldn't be seen associating with someone like Matilda, but she could be benevolent and have someone else bring it to her. If no one else would, she'd ask Lou or Homer to take it to the lady.

Scarlett fanned herself. It was hot in the house. She collected some water and poured some into her basin and then brought it into her room. Her mud-laden dress was filthy. She'd have to wash it herself. There were no sisters to bribe in Silver Falls. She unfastened the dress and stepped out of it, and then she began to wash herself.

It felt so good to get the grime and sweat from the day off of her. She had forgotten a towel, but she'd make due. She went into her trunk and took out a shift, and at that moment, a noise near her door froze her in place. Someone was there. Holding the shift against her front, she turned around.

Dillon stared at her with appreciation in his eyes.

"A decent man would have turned away immediately."

"Perhaps, but I couldn't take my eyes off you, Scarlett. Your skin is beautiful." He didn't look repentant one bit.

"The least you could do is apologize," she snapped.

"I'm not in the least bit sorry. You standing there is the best sight I've seen in a very long time." His gaze traveled from her bare feet up to the top of her head.

"Please go." She was almost in tears. She wasn't a plaything, and she deserved some respect.

"Aww, honey, I'm sorry. I'll go change and give you your privacy. I didn't mean to upset you." He walked away before she could reply.

Quickly, she went to the door and closed it. Her hands shook as she tried to clothe herself. She was too rattled to button the front of her dress, and she couldn't face him half dressed. What could she do? He was bound to come for her soon.

She didn't have long to wait. He lightly knocked on the door.

"Scarlett, are you coming out? I really am sorry."

"I–I can't." She hated the way her voice wavered.

The door slowly opened. "Please, we can talk about it. I…" He gazed at her and stopped talking. He walked to her and sat on the bed. Next, he pulled her between his knees and buttoned her up without looking. How he managed, she didn't know. He stood and kissed her forehead. "I didn't mean to upset you."

"I know," she whispered. Her stomach flipped. It was strange.

"Come, I'll make dinner," He took her hand and led her to the kitchen.

"You'll make dinner? When will we be hiring some help around here?"

He dropped her hand and faced her. "Help?"

"Yes, a cook or a housekeeper. Of course with a house this big both are probably required."

His brow furrowed. "Isn't that what a wife does? I know you didn't grow up with servants."

"But you can certainly afford them. You have Homer and Lou down at the smithy."

He closed his eyes and took a deep breath. When he opened them, he did not look pleased. "They are apprentices. I provide them with a house to live in and food, and I pay them a wage. Most importantly, I am teaching them my craft. It is not at all like having servants."

She folded her arms in front of her. "So, you married me so I can be your servant." She couldn't help the outrage in her voice.

"I married you so you could be my wife and give me children. I had hoped for the best. I planned for us to be friends at least." He shook his head and grabbed a cast iron frying pan he'd made. "I'm making dinner tonight because I thought you might be tired, but don't think I won't expect you to do it in the future."

He put the fire grate over the hot coals and set the pan on top of it. Next, he fried up bacon and scrambled some eggs. He dished the food out on two plates and handed hers to her. After that, he went and sat at the table. That morning, she had taken little notice of how well-crafted that table was. Where had he gotten it?

Swallowing hard, she joined him, though her appetite had fled. She'd been duped by him. He had the biggest house in the whole town. She expected more, so much more. She glanced up from her plate and found him staring at her.

"Is something else wrong?" she asked, using her haughty voice.

"Why didn't you read my letters? I never once mentioned

servants. In fact, I asked if you were up to taking care of a big place. You assured me you could."

She cocked her right brow at him. "Yes with servants I could. I feel tricked into marrying you."

"Is that so?" His voice was too calm, but she wasn't afraid of him.

"Yes that's so. I expected someone respectable, not someone covered in soot all the time. I expected a furnished house with live-in help. I expected to be the most sought-out woman in town, but that one I can work on. I'm not even sure I'd be a good mother. Kids have sticky fingers that ruin dresses." She lifted her chin and stared right back at him.

His eyes grew wide as he threw his napkin on the table and stood. "You sure had your father fooled. He sang your praises. Now I'm stuck with a spoiled brat who lied about everything. You think you have it bad? I'm saddled with an unpleasant, rude, and childish liar. How do you think I feel? I was set for a new beginning, a wonderful beginning, but I'm stuck with you instead." He walked out the front door, closing it behind him with a heavy thud.

Stunned, she jumped up and raced to the window, surprised to see him saddle Coal and ride off. Any other person would have backed down from her and given in. In a huff, she walked back to the kitchen. She ate her food and left the dirty dishes right where they were. She'd be no man's maid.

Later, in bed, she waited and listened, but he never came home.

CHAPTER FOUR

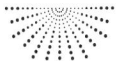

It poured the next morning, trapping her in the house. She found some bread and ate that. The dishes were still where they'd been left the night before. She wasn't about to clean them. Instead, she grabbed her knitting and sat on the only sofa in the house, pulled a blanket up over her and continued to make the scarf. She must have fallen asleep because the next thing she knew, she heard stomping going on in the kitchen. Dillon had returned. She sighed.

Hopefully, he'd learned the error of his ways. Of course, he'd have to apologize to her before she'd talk to him.

She waited, but she only heard him leave the kitchen and go into his bedroom. Oh, but he was a stubborn man. Well, he wouldn't win. She started to smile until she spotted him near the front door, a valise in hand.

He stopped and turned toward her. "I'll be staying in town. If chasing me out of my own house was what you had in mind, then you succeeded. I'll cancel the party Saturday. I don't see how you would need me, but you know where I work." He opened the door.

"Will you be sleeping there too?"

"No, I've had many offers over the years." He walked out the door and slammed it behind him.

Now what? This wasn't supposed to happen. He was supposed to succumb to her beauty and give her whatever she wanted. She blew out a frustrated breath. Well, he'd miss her soon enough. He'd be back the next day, she was sure of it.

After he was gone, she stood on the front porch and watched the rain. It matched her gloomy mood. A small cry came from the side of the house. She hesitated for a moment, not wanting to get wet, but when another pitiful cry came, she trudged through the mud and found the sweetest calico kitten with her paw stuck in the mud.

Squatting down, Scarlett petted the tiny thing, and was surprised when the kitten didn't hiss at her. She'd never had a way with animals like the rest of her family. Should she take the cat inside? Would Dillon want a cat in the house? Did she care? Tilting her head, she smiled at the calico. "How would you like to come live with me? I have to warn you, not too many people or animals seem to like me." She lifted the small ball of fur into her arms. "Tell you what, we'll give it a trial run. *I'll* never make you leave, but if you decide you can't stand me you can leave on your own."

A lump formed in her throat. Leave, just like everyone else in her life. The kitten was filthy but for once, Scarlett didn't care about the dirt.

DILLON'S back hurt so much from four nights of sleeping on the floor, he finally sent Lou across the street to see about a ready-made mattress and a pile of blankets. If they didn't have a ready-made one, Lou was to offer to pay them to make him a mattress.

He tried to put his wife out of his mind, but he worried about her. It was stupid; she surely wasn't worrying about him. There was plenty of food at the house, provided she could actually cook. It amazed him how fast word got around town that they were living apart. He refused to comment on it. What was he supposed to say? His wife was a selfish brat? No, it was better to keep his mouth shut.

The evenings were the worst. He mourned the death of his dreams. There would be no love or children, and at this rate he'd need to build himself another house to live in. But tonight, at least, he'd have something to sleep on in his office.

Lolly had been a life saver, supplying him with three great meals a day. But he hated the questions in her eyes whenever she came to the smithy. He needed to make it known that he wouldn't break the vows he'd taken before God.

A brisk wind cut through his shop, drawing a shiver. It was unseasonably cold that day as it had poured again. Was she warm enough? He needed to slap himself on the head for even thinking about her. He wasn't going to get her servants, now or ever.

Work was done for the day and he'd eaten and then brought back the plate to Lolly. Now he sat and designed. He'd started by working out the details on some better tools, but his thoughts had drifted to his new house. The door opened, and he smiled when Terry walked in with a whiskey jug in one hand.

"Thought you might need a drink or two," Terry said as he grabbed two cups off a shelf.

"Good to see you. I could use a drink. It's been...well I don't remember a worse week." He accepted the offered cup and took a swig. The full bodied whiskey went down his throat nice and smooth. So much better than the rotgut most places sold.

Terry sat in a chair facing Dillon's desk. "The rumor mill is turning quickly. Too bad the saw mill doesn't work as fast. Let's see, Melly is certain you will put Scarlett aside and marry her. Elda ordered a new dress just like the one Scarlett was wearing, and Lolly is said to be very hopeful. Those are just the ones I know about. Some of the women think you are plain mean, and most of the men want you to stick to your guns."

"What about you?"

Terry shrugged one shoulder. "I don't even know the facts, but I'm always on your side."

Dillon smiled. "She insists on servants and she doesn't want kids. She thinks I tricked her about the servants, but I wrote in one of my letters and asked if she could handle taking care of a big house. She admitted she didn't even read the letters, she just skimmed them. I think she wanted a banker." He gestured at his work-soiled clothing. "I'm too dirty for her highness."

Terry poured more whiskey into their cups. "That bad, huh? You'd have to go to another town to find servants. Well, actually, maybe a few of the women whose husbands are lumberjacks might be interested."

"She wants live-in help," Dillon sneered. "And she left the dirty dishes on the table as if she was beneath washing them."

"What do you plan to do? I heard you've been sleeping in your office. You're welcome to stay at the ranch."

Dillon shook his head. "Thanks, but I want to be close in case she needs me. I'm going to build a house for myself right next to her. I picked that view and worked hard until I had the money to buy the land."

"You always did have a good sense of humor." Terry chuckled.

"I mean it. She wasn't raised with servants, and she said she was good with children. This whole marriage is a lie. She doesn't know how to tell the truth." Dillon's anger grew.

"She's young. She just has a lot to learn. I'd just give it some time."

"I haven't bedded her yet. I was being a gentleman, thinking to give her time to get to know me. By golly, I won't be led around by some woman who thinks she can tell me what to do!"

"Perhaps a few days alone will change her attitude," Terry suggested with a shrug. "With all the rain she wouldn't be able to get to town. Has anyone checked on her?"

Warmth flooded Dillon's face. "No. I've been too mad to think about it. I suppose I should go up there tomorrow and check on her. Maybe I can just look through the window to see."

Terry laughed. "Don't let her pretty face turn you into a coward."

Sighing, Dillon shook his head. "She is beautiful, isn't she?"

"Pretty on the outside. Now you need to find the goodness on the inside."

Dillon wiped his hand over his face. "That might take a while."

THE LONGER HE IGNORED HER, the madder she got. No one ignored Scarlett Settler—make that Stahl. If she'd had a way to get a message to her pa, she'd have done it. The rain had stopped but it would take forever for the mud to dry.

She sat at the kitchen table staring at a pair of old cowboy boots of Dillon's. The kitten, now named Missy, was sleeping on top of the toe of one boot. Scarlett assessed their size.

Maybe if she stuffed the toe area she'd be able to wear them to town. She'd have to rig up a way to get them out of the mud once they got sucked in, of course.

What kind of man leaves his wife alone for days?

She never should have left her family. She missed them so much. She didn't realize how much she leaned on all of them until she had come to Silver Falls. She hadn't realized that she'd be so lonely. Missy was a good listener, but it wasn't the same.

That was it. No man ignored her. She'd just go to town and see where he'd been spending the nights. She'd been told there wasn't a free room in the town. Was Dillon a scoundrel? She didn't even know him.

Garbed in her most serviceable dress, she looked in the mirror. The dress was finer than any she'd seen worn in this backward town, and it would be a muddy mess by the time she made it down the hill. But she had no choice. Next, she stuffed her rolled up stockings into the toe of the boots until they fit her.

Looking around, she found some rope. Her plan was to run a length of rope under the boots and hold onto the ends so if they got stuck she could get them out by pulling up on the rope. She smiled, she was so clever. She then borrowed one of Dillon's belts and used it to hike her dress up about six inches. At least the hem wouldn't be muddy.

She picked up her kitten and kissed her nose. "I'll be back in a bit. You'll be just fine." Missy meowed when Scarlett put her on the bed.

Grabbing her reticule and cape, she started out on her journey. She had a letter to her pa in her pocket, asking him to come get her.

As soon as she stepped off the porch, her boot got stuck. Her plan with the rope worked great. She was going to be exhausted by the time she got there, but it would be worth it.

From the top of the hill, she could see most of the town, but it was the rich green of the trees beyond the town that held her attention. Too bad she wouldn't get a chance to see the falls. Imagine, ten falls within walking distance.

Twice she almost landed on her backside, but she'd been able to regain her balance each time. She was glad to see her hem was still mud free. As soon as she stepped on the boardwalk she'd put her contraptions in her reticule. She had just enough money for postage. After smoothing down her dress, she pulled her shoulders back and walked to the store. The bell above the door jingled when she entered.

Dinah Bains' brows rose before she hurried Scarlett's way.

"Oh, my dear. Are you all right? I hear your husband left you. I always thought of Dillon as a son, but not when he treats a woman the way he has."

"I'm just fine, thank you." Her heart skipped a beat. Everyone knew! Just like before, she was the subject of gossip.

Melly hurried down the steps. "Hi, Scarlett. How's married life been?" She sneered.

Dillon should have married Melly. She was pretty, and they already knew each other. He wouldn't have left her alone at the house even if she was catty.

"I'm fine." She turned toward Dinah. "I have a letter I'd like to post. Can I take care of it here?"

Dinah nodded. "Yes, let's go to the back counter, and I'll be happy to help."

Scarlett followed her. There were was a surprisingly large collection of items for sale.

Dinah went behind the counter, and Scarlett handed her the letter. Dinah looked at it. "That'll be four cents."

Scarlett cocked her right brow. "I thought it was three cents."

"It's four cents." Dinah stared her down.

Rummaging through her bag once again, she confirmed that she had no more than three cents. The bell on the door jingled, but she didn't pay it much mind.

"I only have three cents," she said as dismay stole over her.

Dinah shrugged her shoulders. "Sorry. I can mail it when you have the correct amount."

Scarlett's stomach dropped. It would be faster to walk home then to find a cent. Troubled, she tried to think of what to do. She fingered the silver locket her ma and pa had given her. Taking it off, she laid it on the counter. "How much would you give me for this?"

Dinah snatched it up and examined it. She opened the locket and frowned. "Who are these people?"

"My parents. They gave me the necklace as a wedding present." Her heart grew heavy. It was crazy to sell the fine locket. "Never mind. I don't want to sell it." She reached her hand out expecting Dinah to give it back.

Instead, Dinah stamped the letter and put the necklace in a drawer. "All set."

"What do you mean all set? That necklace was worth more than a cent. You took my last three cents and an expensive necklace in exchange for postage?"

"It's called business, dear. You have a good day now." She walked away from the counter and hurried up the steps.

Scarlett moved to follow but she was suddenly blocked by Melly. "We live up there, and you're not invited. Like my ma said, good day."

Scarlett turned to go and realized that Lolly had come in. "Hello, Lolly."

Lolly nodded and pushed past her toward the counter.

Scarlett swallowed hard as she left the store. She stared at the smithy across the street. Dillon was hard at work, and she wished she could go and talk to him or just sit and watch him but that would never do. She walked to the end of the wooden walkway, put her ropes and belt to good use, and stepped off into the mud. She was going to see the falls before she left.

She walked down the wet, dirt road and then turned onto a well-beaten path into the woods. It was like being in a different world. The foliage was greener, and the air smelled sweeter. The tall trees created a wonderful canopy, and the ground wasn't as muddy. The thundering of the water beckoned, and she walked faster, bursting free of the dense woods after a time. Stunned she stopped in place.

What a sight to behold. She stood at the base of the falls in awe. God was responsible for such beauty, and it humbled her. Dillon had said there were ten falls in all. The path led farther north, but she was content for now to just sit on a big rock and watch the water fall over the edge far above and come crashing down.

She was glad no one had taken this land to be their own. It was too spectacular to be kept by one person. The color of the water tumbling down was white and blue with a hint of green. She looked closely as the rock she sat upon and was pleased when she made out a carving of a man with a bow and arrow etched into it. So this used to be Indian land; somehow it saddened her that they were taken away from such a beautiful place and put on a reservation. She'd like to ask Dillon more about them, but would she ever have the opportunity?

Her stomach growled. How stupid of her. She hadn't thought to pack anything to eat or drink. Well, there was plenty of water in front of her. She walked closer and saw a ledge behind the falls that couldn't be seen from the front. Intrigued, she carefully walked behind the cascading water and laughed. Who would have ever imagined such a thing?

One part of the rock ledge jutted closer to the falls. She

stood there and filled her cupped hands with water then put them to her lips and sipped. It slaked her thirst. How amazing. She walked back the way she came, wet from the mist. At least she had gotten to see it before she left.

Sadness encased her as she stood watching the falls again. Life certainly hadn't gone the way she'd thought. If she was going to be talked about, she'd rather have the protection of her parents. Dillon had nothing to offer her. He didn't even like her.

After a deep sigh, she started to walk back to town and then up the hill to her lonely existence. In a week, possibly two, her pa would be there. She needed his comforting arms around her. He made her feel safe, but it had taken her a long time to learn to trust her adoptive parents. Up until she'd met them, it seemed that everyone she loved either died or just left.

She hadn't even gotten a chance to know Dillon but he'd already left her. She had tried to be a proper lady. She practiced good posture and how to cock just one brow. The brow stopped many in their tracks. Her manners were impeccable as was her taste in clothing. She wore her hair stylishly and tried to always have a smile on her face. She'd tried so hard to be a perfect woman that everyone would seek out as a friend. She was perfect wife material. What man wouldn't want her on his arm? She could be the cream of society given the chance.

Shaking her head, she sighed. Her efforts weren't appreciated in Silver Falls, especially by Dillon. He had too many other options being flaunted in front of him. He'd chosen her but now was sorry. He obviously wished he'd have chosen another. Probably Melly.

This time when she reached the walkway she didn't even bother to step up on it. Instead, she made her way down the muddy street and headed up the hill.

"Well I'll be," Homer commented as he stared outside.

"What is Mrs. Stahl doing here?" Lou asked.

"Looks like she's heading back up the hill. Hope she doesn't slip," Homer said as he checked another finished piece off the list.

Dillon stepped outside. He must have missed her. He headed to the back door and opened it. There she was, struggling to make it up the hill, but she was doing it. He went back inside.

"Lou, take the wagon and get Mrs. Stahl home before she breaks her neck."

Lou turned a bit red but did as he was bade.

Had she run out of food? He hadn't set up an account for her to charge to at the store. Maybe she was trying to hire a maid. He shook his head. She needed to grow up. He'd order the wood for his new house later that day. He was almost finished with the plans, indoor water pump and all. His pencil was down to the nub. He took off his leather apron and put his hat on. "I'll be at the store."

He didn't wait for a response but hiked through the mud to the opposite walkway. He opened the door to the familiar ring of the overhead bell. The first person he saw was Melly. He inwardly groaned. He still couldn't believe she'd bought a wedding dress. He'd hardly talked to her except to do business at the store.

"Miss Bains," he greeted. He tipped his hat to her and went toward the back. He picked up a pencil, a piece of paper, and an envelope. He needed to send a letter to Smitty, but he didn't know what to write.

"Hello, Dillon," Mrs. Bains greeted. "My, what a lucky day; first your wife and now you."

"I just want the pencil, paper, and envelope."

"A letter? That's what the Missus was here to do." Dinah smiled as though she had a secret.

Dillon didn't want to take the bait, but he was too curious. "A letter to her family no doubt."

"Why yes." Dinah commented. "Melly, could you take care of Mr. Stahl for me? I have something on the stove that requires my attention. Good to see you again, Dillon." She whisked up the steps.

Melly was behind the counter in no time. "Did you want to write the letter here so you won't have to make another trip back?"

"No, I'll write it later. How much do I owe you?"

"Four cents sounds about right. Too bad Scarlett didn't have but three cents on her." Melly fingered the necklace that hung around her neck.

Dillon's mouth went dry as fury raced through him. "Isn't that my wife's necklace?"

"How can you call her a wife? You don't even live together. She must be a real shrew to have driven you away." Melly's smile turned cunning. "You know if she died you could remarry."

He waited for a moment to calm himself. "You didn't answer my question. Is that my wife's necklace?" His voice thundered. Melly was lucky he wasn't a violent man.

"She didn't have enough to send the letter," Melly said defensively.

"How much did you give her for the necklace? It's expensive and hand crafted." She hesitated. "I asked how much!"

"A cent. She had three cents and to mail a letter is four cents."

"Since when? I only pay three cents when I post a letter." He put his hand in his pocket and took out two cents. "Here I'll pay double what you paid and don't try to give me a hard time. I'll get the sheriff. This is robbery."

Her hands shook as she took the necklace off and handed it to him. She scooped up the two cents and turned her back on him.

He took his purchases and left. There was no reason to take advantage of Scarlett. He stared down at the necklace. It was very intricate, and it had taken him a long time to make. He'd sent it to Smitty to give to Scarlett as a goodbye present. He was almost to the smithy when he heard Dinah calling out to him.

"A trade is a trade. Besides, you don't know how much that trinket is worth. I bet it isn't even real silver."

Dillon turned around and strode to where Dinah stood. "It's made of pure grade silver and the intricate pattern took a very long time to make. I should know. I made it!"

Her eyes widened. "I, well, I assumed—" she sputtered.

"That's the problem. Instead of giving her the real price to post a letter, you charged her a cent more and then you had the gall to trade this necklace for a cent? You must have known how wrong it was. Taking advantage of your customers is just plain criminal."

"Humph, I'll await your apology, Dillon." Dinah turned and walked back into her store.

Were all the women in town loco or what? He'd had enough. He whistled loudly when he spotted Lou coming down the hill and gestured for him to come his way. Scarlett would probably want her necklace back.

CHAPTER FIVE

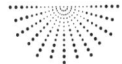

*D*illon put his hand in his pocket to be sure he had the necklace. It had been a long day and he needed to give it back to Scarlett. He didn't necessarily want to see her but she deserved to have her property returned. She probably didn't even know he'd made it. He'd told Smitty not to say anything. He'd wanted the necklace to be a gift from Smitty and Lynn. He figured it would be a hard thing to leave home and marry a stranger.

He rubbed the back of his neck. Yes, marrying a stranger was hard. He flicked the lines, urging the horses to pull the wagon up the hill. That was the one drawback of living in Silver Falls, the rain. His stomach clenched as he arrived at the house.

Would she welcome him or throw something at him? He liked that she was a strong woman, but she was unpredictable, and since he didn't know her, he had no idea how she'd react when he went through the door. He put on the brake and climbed down the wagon. He didn't plan to stay long.

A set of muddy footprints tracked over the porch, and he

furrowed his brow. They were too big to be hers. He quickly went into the house, hoping she was all right. He had his hand on his gun, ready for anything.

She was sitting on the floor in front of the fire playing with a cat. A cat? He relaxed. There was no danger.

Scarlett gathered the cat to her and stared at him. A flicker of fear grew in her eyes. "Did something happen? I mean the way you slammed in here."

She looked so very beautiful. Half her hair was falling down, and he found it enchanting. He felt a tug at his heart, but he instantly ignored it. "Everything is fine. I just saw a man's footprints on the front porch, and it alarmed me."

She smiled. "I wore your boots to town. I had to stuff the toes with socks to make them fit." She rubbed her cheek against the kitten.

"I heard you'd been in town today."

"Yes, I mailed a letter to my parents asking them to come get me. I should be out of your way in a few days. This is Missy. I found her crying with her paw stuck in the mud. I'm keeping her." She lifted her chin. "I'm taking her with me when I go."

"You wrote to Smitty? Don't you think it childish to drag your parents into our business?" He took off his hat and threw it on the table.

"They said if anything was amiss I should write to them. I think you hating me is reason enough." Her voice rose with each word. She stood up and walked over until she stood toe to toe with him.

"I never said I hated you," he denied, shaking his head.

Her eyes glittered. "What am I supposed to think? You are not pleased with me. You moved out and have never inquired after me."

Guilt washed over him at the hurt on her face. He didn't know what he was supposed to do. He glanced around. The house was nice and clean. He bet she eventually washed the dishes too.

"You're pleasing to look at. You're intelligent and..." He tried to think of other qualities she had and came up blank. "I don't know you well enough to know if you have other pleasing qualities or not."

Her jaw dropped and she set Missy down. "Then it's a good thing I sent a letter to my parents. I know when I'm not wanted. You don't consider me an asset at all. I'm just a bother. Besides Melly and Lolly have made it clear *they* want to marry you." She turned and went back to the fire.

"I couldn't choose between a few of the women here, so I figured I'd order up a bride. I had hoped for one who was useful." He quickly shut his mouth. It wouldn't do to say hateful things. "I didn't mean to say that. I'm aggravated by the situation. I'm just tired."

A tear trailed down her face when she turned to face him. "My sister, Mia said I'd get my comeuppance someday. She said someone would put me in my place. I thought Dexter had done that, but you're worse. Too bad you didn't walk away before we were married. I bet there are plenty of people who are married yet live apart." She brushed the tear away and the next one too.

"I wanted children. I wanted a family. I won't get those things if we live apart. I wouldn't plan on you going anywhere. I'm your husband, and what I say goes. I'm going to write to Smitty and tell him not to come." He pulled the necklace out of his pocket. "I got this back for you." He went to her and secured it around her neck.

With a gasp, she fingered the heart and then whispered, "Thank you."

"Well I have the horses waiting outside. I need to take them back to the livery."

"I'm to be your prisoner? Don't worry you won't need a

guard. I don't have the means to get home." She turned her back on him again.

He watched as her back stiffened. He'd hoped... He didn't even know what he hoped for. Deep down he had expected her to come running to him, so glad to see him that their differences wouldn't matter.

He picked up his hat and walked out the door. He regretted the way things were between them. After he climbed onto the wagon, he turned the horses and went back down. He had a letter to write. The post wouldn't be picked up for a few days. Maybe he could talk Melly into giving him Scarlett's letter. No, he decided. He didn't want to be dishonest.

THE HAMMERING and sawing could be heard at the house. It had started a week ago. Scarlett watched as the men built a new building in town. It looked like a hotel. She frowned and then yawned. She didn't sleep much at night since Dillon had been to see her. He was good at one thing, ignoring her. She went back inside and started to make some soup. A piece of carrot fell onto the floor, and Missy immediately began to play with it. At least with the cat around, she didn't have to lie in bed alone.

She heard what sounded like applause and yahoos, and hurried outside again. A wagon filled with women had rolled into town. Her heart dropped. Even from up on her hill she could tell by the gaudy colors of their hair that they were fallen women. Which one would Dillon pick? She'd heard plenty of stories about husbands stepping out on their wives.

She'd hoped that her parents would have come to get her by now. She'd considered the possibility that they'd written back but that would mean another trip to town. Dread filled her but she'd best go now, before word of Dillon and one of those women became gossip. It would just be another thing for Dinah and Melly Bains to throw in her face.

She changed her dress and put on Dillon's boots again. She wished she had a pair of her own but that wasn't to be. The ground wasn't wet but the mud had hardened leaving wheel impressions in it. She'd need to be mindful so she didn't trip or turn her ankle. Peering into the mirror she hardly recognized the sad woman staring back at her. Her hair was tangled but she didn't care, she just covered it with a bonnet.

"Missy, I'll be back in a bit."

The kitten rolled into a ball in front of the fireplace and promptly fell asleep. With a hint of a smile on her lips, Scarlett started out.

The raised ridges from the horses' hooves and the wagon wheels made walking worse than she'd imagined. Before Dexter had jilted her, she used to love going to the store and buying something, anything. Even a piece of candy had once gladdened her heart, but now she was penniless. Would there be a letter for her? She decided to be hopeful. She'd already spent enough time being miserable.

Her arrival into town went unnoticed by the men who were greeting the soiled doves. She quickly went into the store and was dismayed to find Dillon talking to Melly. Melly had the brightest of smiles on her face until she spotted Scarlett.

"What do you want?" she asked harshly.

Dillon flirting with Melly left Scarlett speechless.

"I asked if there something you wanted?"

Scarlett blinked and raised her head while she pulled her shoulders back. "Yes, I've come to inquire if a letter is here for me." She didn't dare glance at Dillon. Her heart was already in pieces.

"Yes, it came yesterday. I gave it to Dillon. Didn't he take it up to you?" Melly laughed.

Scarlett wasn't about to ask Dillon for it. She turned and walked out of the store, down the boardwalk and up the hill. Blinded by tears, she tripped. She got up and wanted to cry out in pain. Her ankle had rolled and it was excruciating to put her weight on it. Her knee and the inside of her thigh pained her too. She was on her own so she limped along, biting her bottom lip until it bled.

As soon as she got close to the house, she dropped to her knees and crawled to the porch. She managed to open the door, and she kept crawling until she was next to a wooden chair. She'd thought to pull herself up, but her energy was gone. Tears streamed down her face as she loudly sobbed. Her parents weren't coming. She didn't need to read the letter.

How would she manage by herself? At least she had enough soup to last her a few days. She'd hauled water that morning. Taking a shaky breath, she managed to stop her tears. She'd have more energy after she rested. She managed to get the boots off and lay down on the floor.

Why hadn't Dillon said a word to her in the store? He allowed Melly to treat her like dirt. If she'd ever held onto any hope for her and Dillon, it was gone now. She needed to make some money to get through. She sewed beautiful dresses. Perhaps she could tone down her dresses for the women of the town and sell them. A sigh escaped her lips. She was too upset to think straight. She closed her eyes and felt Missy curl up next to her. Then Scarlett's eyelids became heavy and she fell asleep.

"MELLY, she is my wife and I expect everyone, including you, to treat her with respect. Now I have to go and smooth down her ruffled feathers."

Melly cast her glance downward. "If I had known you'd have to go to the house, I wouldn't have said a word." She looked up at him with a hopeful smile. "Forgive me?"

"Sure. You didn't know. Now, as I was saying, I don't think putting bars on your bedroom window is necessary. Those women don't want to bother you. They certainly won't try to break in."

"But they will attract undesirable men who just might. If they get a good look at me, I won't have a safe moment."

He swallowed back his smile. "Talk to your father about it. If he wants them, have him come over to the smithy. I need to go after my wife."

"I wouldn't bother. She didn't even look at you."

"I feel it my duty to keep trying. We did say our vows in church, and that's the same as saying them to God. I'll see you later." He began to walk away.

"When?"

"When what?" Dillon asked.

"When will I see you? You could come for dinner."

He gave her a gentle smile. "That wouldn't be right." He walked outside and looked up the hill. It was a nice enough day, so he'd walk home. First, he went to the smithy and let Homer know where to find him, and then off he went.

He frowned at the rough road. Scarlett was probably wearing his boots again. He shook his head until he spotted blood on the ground. Darn, she must have fallen. He hurried up the hill reasoning that if she could walk up to the house it couldn't be that bad. Then he saw blood again in front of the house, going up the steps and over the threshold. The door had been left open.

"Scarlett?" he called. He walked farther into the house and found her on the floor. Panic beset him as he knelt at her side. He brushed the side of her face with the back of his hand. "Scarlett?" Her fluttering eyelashes calmed him a bit.

"Dillon? What are you doing here?" Her brow furrowed as she stared up at him.

"I thought to check on you. There was blood on the road up here."

She nodded. "I fell. Scraped my knee and turned my ankle. I crawled the rest of the way to the house."

He scooped her up off the floor. She was lighter than before. Hadn't she been eating? He walked to the living room and set her on the sofa. Then he lifted her skirts up past her knee. Her mouth formed an O. She'd have to just be fine with showing her legs.

"This is more than a scrape. It's a gash with pebbles stuck in it. I'll get the supplies."

"Supplies?"

"I'll need to clean it. Did you say your ankle hurt?"

Nodding, she seemed apprehensive. "It's going to hurt isn't it?"

He walked into the kitchen and gathered what he'd need. He hoped he didn't need to stitch it up. "I'm not going to lie. It'll hurt plenty. Now I want you to promise to lie still and not to grab my hand."

Her eyes grew wide. "I promise," she squeaked.

He grabbed a cloth and wet it. Next, he dabbed at her cut until he could see the small pieces of rock. Taking his tweezers in hand, he carefully extracted the first pebble. Sweat beaded on her forehead, but she didn't scream. At least not yet. Taking a deep breath, he removed the rest, and there were plenty. He decided to bandage it and see how it healed. He didn't want her to endure the pain of his stitching if it could be avoided.

"I'll wrap your ankle now."

She just nodded. Her hands moved, catching his attention. They were bleeding too.

Dillon took one than the other into his hands and examined them. She must have clenched her fists so hard her nails dug in and broke the skin. He cleaned her palms. Next, he bandaged her ankle. From the amount of swelling, it was a bad sprain. At least it wasn't broken.

He sat back on his haunches and brushed her hair away from her face. "You won't be able to walk on it for a good while." He tried to sound sympathetic. "I brought your letter." He reached into his pocket and pulled it out. He handed it to her.

"It's fine. I don't need to read it. I already know they aren't coming. If they were, they wouldn't have sent a letter. They were probably glad to be rid of me." Tears filled her eyes.

"I doubt—" He saw an animal running toward Scarlett's bedroom. It ran so fast he wasn't able to make out what it was. He jumped up. "I need to get an animal that must have come in when the door was left open. Probably a raccoon or something."

She jutted out her chin as though ready to fight with him. "My kitten, Missy. You must have scared her."

"I forgot you had that darn kitten." He frowned.

"Why should you remember? You're never here. She sleeps with me. It gets lonely up on this hill. You don't even have one single book to read. Besides, Missy likes me." She turned her head away from him.

Instead of storming into the bedroom, he walked slowly and then stood at the doorway. Sure enough, it was her calico kitten. He surprised himself by smiling. The cat meowed as he approached and gave him the weakest, sweetest hiss. He quickly scooped her up and petted her. "Let's get you back to where you belong."

When he walked out of the bedroom, he was horrified to find Scarlett struggling to her feet. "What in tarnation are you doing?"

"You're not getting rid of Missy!" Tears began to flow down her cheeks.

She could take all the pain it took for him to tend to her yet she cried about a silly cat.

"I was just bringing her out here to you." He helped her back onto the couch with one hand while holding Missy in the other. "Here." He placed the kitten in her arms and was rewarded with a watery smile.

She was right. He didn't know her, and it was plain she had no idea he loved animals. He'd have to find someone to take care of her. His head began to ache. With all the talk in town, he doubted he'd be able to find anyone willing.

"I'll move back into the house. I'll need someone here to see to you. I could ask Lolly."

"No! I'd rather struggle on my own than to have Lolly here. She has designs on you."

He released a sigh. "I think she did until I got married. She's not the type to step out with a married man."

Scarlett gave him a look as if to say he was a fool. "You'll have to get one of my sisters to come."

He rubbed his jaw. "You're not going back home when you're healed up. You are my wife."

"They don't want me back."

The stricken expression she wore tugged at his heart. "They probably just want you to stay with me is all. If we tried, we might be able to make this work between us. We'll just have to try is all."

Why her frown bothered him so much he wasn't sure but it did. "I don't think we have time to wait for one of your sisters to come out. You stay put. I'll grab you some water and food and then see who I can find."

He felt the heat of her stare as she watched his every move. Finally, after making sure she was comfortable, he leaned over and kissed her on the forehead. She tried to pull her head away but she didn't have enough room on the sofa to pull back very far. "I'll be back in a bit. You rest, and I'll see about finding you a book."

"A book would be good." She looked so tired.

"I'll get you something for the pain. We don't have a doctor, but the Bains have supplies stocked." He gave her one last long look before he left.

He carefully avoided the ruts and walked down the hill, mulling over the possibilities. Who would be willing to take care of Scarlett? It was sad to say but he didn't want to take care of her either. Though she hadn't been a brat when he tended to her. Maybe those days alone had made an impact on her. He continued walking. More likely it was the fact that her parents didn't seem inclined to come for her that made her hold her tongue.

He smiled. It was hard to imagine she still had the cat. He'd have thought the fear of cat fur on her clothes would have kept her from bringing it inside. He stood in front of the general store. Perhaps Melly could... He inwardly groaned. Melly and Scarlett would pull each other's hair out. He'd have to come up with another solution.

The bell rang as he entered the store, and the whole place suddenly grew silent as a group of women all turned and stared at him. His face heated. Melly was probably gossiping about him and his wife. They parted as he made his way to the counter.

Melly smiled brightly. "What can I get for you, Dillon? Two visits in one day? People will talk, you know." She tried to sound teasing, but he knew it to be the truth.

"I need bandages, a new sewing kit for stitches, and laudanum."

"Did Homer or Lou get hurt?"

"No, Scarlett fell on her way up to the house. She sprained her ankle and ended up with a big gash on her leg."

Melly tried to look concerned, but she couldn't hide her smile. "I do hope her leg isn't too unsightly. Scarring is most likely." She pretended to shudder.

He tried to ignore her, but anger began burning inside him. "Do you have books proper for a woman?"

"Women don't read anything except for poetry," Dinah Bains informed him as she walked down the stairs. "I'm afraid we don't have anything for your wife."

Dillon pretended he didn't hear her. He went to a shelf where books were kept and looked through a couple that looked to be in good condition still. He picked out two and brought them back to the counter. "I'll take these too."

Dinah pursed her lips. "If she's that bad off, you should ship her home. I know her parents won't come get her, but there's nothing stopping you from sending her away."

He waited for Melly to box his purchases. "Put it on my tab." He picked up the crate. "I'll just say this once. This is my wife you are so callously talking about."

"You're the one who moved out," Dinah retorted.

"True, and I see now it was a huge mistake. I'm moving back in. I expect you all to give Scarlett the respect any wife deserves." He turned and walked out of the store. Too bad they were women, he was in the mood to punch someone.

He stepped into the street.

"Dillon! Oh, Dillon can we speak with you?"

He turned and there was Olga and Elda hurrying toward him. He narrowed his eyes. They had both been in the store.

Olga put her hand to her chest as though she was out of breath. "I wanted to see if you needed someone to take care of your wife while you are at work?"

He glanced at Elda who smiled sweetly at him. "Actually, I am. It'll be a live-in position for at least a month, I suspect."

"If we, Elda and I both came to stay Scarlett would want for nothing. I know a little about nursing. I had to take care of my poor father before he died. Truth is, I'm hoping to set aside a little nest egg. It's hard to keep the two of us fed in the winter. Not as many people feel the need for clean clothes when it's cold out."

"I understand. Growing up, winter was always a meager time for my family too. Will an hour give you enough time to pack? I'll send Lou with the wagon if that suits you."

Olga smiled. "That suits us just fine. Thank you so much." Olga and Elda hurried off.

Dillon walked to his smithy, hoping he hadn't just made a mistake.

A FEW HOURS LATER, he packed his own things and walked up to his house. If they weren't screaming at each other when he got there, he'd be happy. Oddly enough, all was quiet when he stepped on the front porch.

He walked into the house and it smelled clean. So far so good. Olga hurried out of the kitchen and greeted him.

"I bet you're hungry. I'll have the food ready soon. Can I get you anything until then?"

He shook his head. "No, I just need a bucket of warm water and a clean basin. I can get them."

"I'll get them for you and leave them in your room while you say hello to your wife."

Hello to your wife? He couldn't help his suspicions Olga was up to something. He studied her face for a moment but she seemed sincere. "Good idea."

Scarlett looked comfortable on the sofa. Someone had put a pillow behind her head, and a blanket over her. He smiled as he caught her gaze and almost fell over when she smiled back.

He put the crate he'd been carrying on the table and then perched himself next to it. "How are you feeling?"

"I'm not sure. I'm in pain but trying to figure out what those two are up to has kept me occupied. They have been oh, so nice to me. Perhaps I'm just cynical, and that's how they really are."

Her eyes were wide, and he'd forgotten just how blue they were. "I brought you something for the pain. I should have sent it along with the Glosses but I wasn't thinking." He unpacked the box and saw her grimace when he took the sewing kit out. "I'm hoping we don't need it."

"Me too." Her gaze unnerved him. It was easy enough to not think of her when he was living at the smithy but now… "Have I ever told you how beautiful you are?"

She quickly glanced away. "What else is in the box?"

He had a lot of making up to do, it seemed. "You said you wanted something to read."

"I heard from Olga Gloss that women around here don't read."

He grinned. "Perhaps most women, but you're not like most women." He handed her the two books.

The excitement on her face was worth the cost of buying them. "Oh my! Ivanhoe by Sir Walter Scott." She examined the book for a moment before she looked at the second book. "Oliver Twist by David Copperfield!" She ran her hands over the cover as though they were precious gifts instead of books.

"I take it you're pleased."

"I've read school books and poetry, but I always longed to read about other places and people and adventure. I don't know which to read first."

Elda walked toward them. "I put your water in your

bedroom, Dillon. Can I help you with anything else?" Her suggestive tone of voice warmed his face.

"No, that's all thank you." He waited until Elda was out of hearing distance. "Don't pay her any mind."

"I'm not worried. She's as ugly as they come."

"I'm going to get washed up." Disappointment filled him. Scarlett hadn't changed a bit. For a very short time, he'd thought her to be a woman of kindness. Elda had always been kind to him, and she wasn't ugly. Plain, maybe, but that didn't matter if the heart was full of goodness.

Once in his room, he took off his shirt and began to wash. Bending over the basin, he splashed water on his face. He reached next to him for the towel and took a step backward when the towel was handed to him.

"Elda, it isn't proper for you to be in here," he admonished as he held the towel in front of his chest.

"It doesn't matter. I'm just an old maid. I doubt anyone would even care."

"Could you please turn your back?"

"Pfft, if it'll make you happy. Besides, you're married." There wasn't one ounce of shame in her voice.

As soon as he put a fresh shirt on, he stared at her back. She stood there straight and tall. Why hadn't she left? "There are plenty of men looking for wives in Silver Falls. Surely you could have your pick of husbands."

She turned and gave him a sad smile. "I was in love once, but he married another." She stared at the floor. "I'd best go and help my mother."

He watched her leave. She sure was a puzzle. He couldn't think of any man she'd shown any interest in. And if the man was now married, she'd need to find someone else. Well, it wasn't his business. He already had one woman to figure out.

Later that evening as he lay alone in his bed, he was still trying to think of a way to get his marriage on track. Scarlett had been nice all evening, and she hadn't complained once. He did see her narrow her eyes at Elda a few times when Elda tried to flirt with him. He smiled. Perhaps Scarlett was jealous. He'd take it slow, but he was going to make their marriage work. There wasn't any other option; he wanted children. Tomorrow was another day, and he'd keep trying to woo her.

CHAPTER SIX

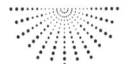

Scarlett tried to keep her thoughts to herself, but that creature made it so very hard. She'd thought Olga the bossy one but Elda was something else. She dominated all conversation when Dillon was home. When he wasn't around she hardly spoke, at least not to Scarlett.

Elda also had an attitude of superiority. She looked down her nose at Scarlett constantly. If Elda had been pretty or intelligent even, Scarlett would have understood but Elda was a plain, stupid rock. She did seem to know a lot about blacksmithing. It was almost as though she'd spent a lot of time with Dillon.

Scarlett needed to show Elda who was boss and who was Dillon's wife. If the girl put her hand on his arm one more time, Scarlett swore she'd scream. It was embarrassing, and Dillon didn't seem to notice. In fact, Dillon didn't have much to say to Scarlett when he was home.

It had been a week, and Scarlett came to the conclusion she'd rather take care of the house and chores herself then have Olga and Elda around. They had even rearranged what little furniture there was. The last straw had been that morning when Elda offered to shave Dillon's face for him.

As soon as she was healed, she planned to kick them down the hill. Missy couldn't be found half the time, and she was sure that Elda locked her in a closet upstairs or something. Her books were her only comfort. Books took her away from the madhouse she lived in.

She wanted to discuss Ivanhoe with Dillon. He'd told her he'd read it a few years ago. But Elda never gave them a minute alone.

"Scarlett, why don't we help you to that chair I just moved in front of the window?" Olga suggested. "You'll have a nice view of the town."

Before she had a chance to answer, both Olga and Elda were there standing her up. The pain was almost beyond bearing as she limped across the room. They were stingy with the laudanum when it suited them unless Dillon was near. Then they dosed her so she'd sleep right after supper. Dillon brushed off her concerns, and it hurt.

After an arduous walk, she sat and leaned back. The view was a nice change. Then she heard the scraping of a chair being pulled next to her.

"Mama is getting us tea. I thought it would be nice for us to sit and have some. I love your dresses. Did you realize we're about the same size? I'm just a bit shorter than you." She smiled at Scarlett.

"You didn't have the audacity to try on my clothes, did you?" Scarlett asked angrily.

"Don't be silly. I think all the pain medicine is making you imagine things that didn't happen. Oh look, the saloon is almost done. I know every man is excited for it to open. When I went to town yesterday, it was all everyone talked about. They said the women were a fresh batch, whatever that means. The whole smithy was talking about it. There is even one girl they call Angel. She sings like an Angel they say. Dillon agreed she had a beautiful voice. You should have seen the look on his face when he talked about her."

Scarlett stared at the big building in town. It never occurred to her that Dillon would go to it. "He's met her?"

"Yes, I heard many of the women visit the smithy at least once a day. Angel is a frequent guest. Melly told me they all fawn over her, including your husband. Melly is concerned that there won't be a single man looking to get married now."

Olga hustled into the room with the tea tray. She poured two cups, then added sugar for Elda and handed them their cups. "Yes, well men stray. It's just something all women have to put up with. It's easiest to just turn a blind eye to the whole thing. It's hard, because your man starts coming home later and later, claiming to have been working late, but you know in your heart where he's been."

"Turn a blind eye? Why I'd kick Dillon out if he behaved like that."

Olga sadly shook her head. "You think that's what you'd do until you realize you own nothing of your own. In fact, your husband owns you. You have no money and nowhere to go. You end up swallowing your pride because you don't want your husband to throw *you* out. It's just the way of things."

Scarlett listened to Olga and sipped her tea until she felt groggy. Blinking her eyes, she couldn't get rid of the cloud of confusion in her mind. All she heard over and over again was that Dillon loved Angel. It was maddening but it made sense.

SHE AWOKE on the couch and looked for the chair next to the window but it wasn't there. It was back where they'd put it days ago when they'd rearranged things. Had she been sitting there looking out the window? Had it all been a dream?

Missy jumped on her chest and demanded to be petted. It was scary not knowing if it had been real or not.

Olga walked toward her. "Oh good you're awake. You've been napping for hours."

"Wasn't I sitting by the window earlier?"

Olga frowned. "Today? No, I would have known if you were. I would have had to help get you there, and we're not supposed to move you unless it's a personal need. Did you have a bad dream?"

"No, I'm fine. Actually, I guess I'd been dreaming. When is the saloon opening?"

"Dillon must have told you he was going there tonight. He told me not to keep supper for him." She tilted her head and smiled. "I bet that's where the dream came from. He must have told you about it."

Scarlett shook her head. "No, he didn't say a word to me about it."

"Well, I wouldn't worry. Dillon is a good man. I'll have supper ready in a bit. Do you need anything?"

"Yes, could you hand me my book?"

Olga looked around for a bit. "Do you know where it is?"

"It was on the side table. I put it there last night." She scooted Missy off of her and sat up. "That's strange, it was right there."

"I'll ask Elda when I see her. She went to town to get a few things. You rest, my dear."

My dear? Scarlett felt as though she was starting to lose her mind. "Yes, I'll do that."

She waited until Olga left before she swung her legs off the sofa. Where was her book? What was going on? Taking a deep breath, she held on to the arm of the sofa and stood on one foot. After scanning the room, she sat back down. Disappointed, she laid her head against the back of the sofa. The saloon was opening tonight? Her dream about sitting at the window chatting with Elda seemed all too real, but a few facts weren't right, so it had to have been a dream. The one thing she did remember was Elda telling her about a woman named Angel that had caught Dillon's eye. Or was that a dream too?

Angel was an unlikely name for a whore. Scarlett sighed. She'd probably be asleep before Dillon got home. She needed to find a way to make things right with him.

Elda walked in, smiling and holding Ivanhoe.

"My book! I've been looking for it." Scarlett reached out her hand expecting Elda to give it to her.

"I've been reading it. I thought you were done."

"You could have asked before you borrowed it."

Elda cocked her head. "I don't know why I'd have to. Dillon told me the books were mine to keep as soon as you were done reading them. You must be an awfully slow reader. I read Oliver Twist already and now I'm reading Ivanhoe."

Scarlett's heart squeezed. "I thought Dillon had given them to me as a gift." Her self-doubt annoyed her.

"I requested these two books when he went to the store. We both decided to let you read them too. I've been collecting books for some time now. None in such a fine condition as the two Dillon gave me though."

Scarlett wasn't in the position to yell, scream, or bully so she just nodded. "I'll read Oliver Twist then."

Elda gave her a look of fake pity. "I took the book home with me today. I guess I could let you borrow it in a few days when I go back to town."

"What am I supposed to do with my free time?"

"I'm sure you have sewing or embroidering to do. Isn't that what women of leisure do? What was it like to grow up rich?" Elda asked with a hint of bitterness in her voice.

"I didn't grow up rich. My parents died, and I was an

orphan until my new parents, Smitty and Lynn Settler took me in. They took in many children whose parents died along the Oregon Trail. They have a big house but with so many children the work is never done." Scarlett sighed. It would be so nice to be back home.

"I just figured since you act so hoity-toity and demanded servants that you were from money. You sure are an odd one. You take the best man around and then make him sleep in town. I hope now that you've lost him, you can see his worth." Keeping the book in her arms she turned and quickly walked away.

Scarlett's jaw dropped. *Lost him?* Had she really lost him? A chill went up her spine. She was doomed to live without love in this awful town. He said their vows were sacred, but what happened when a husband couldn't stand his wife? She didn't understand about the books either. Hope had started to bloom in her heart when he'd handed them to her. But he hadn't intended for her to keep them.

Heat licked at her cheeks. She was such a fool. He didn't care about her. She'd mistakenly thought she was the one in control of their future but he'd already made up his mind. It was just as well to know now. If he really came to know her, he wouldn't like her. No one ever did.

Before the accident, she didn't have to put on airs living with just Missy. It was nice, it was restful, it was truthful, but she didn't know how else to act when other people were around. Her *hoity-toity* attitude was an act perfected by practice. If no one got too close, they couldn't hurt her when they left…and they always left. She'd been more hurt than she'd let on when Dexter jilted her. It wasn't just the humiliation, it was knowing she was unwanted that tore at her.

Here she was once again living in a town where she wasn't considered worth visiting. She'd thought for sure some of the women from town would come to check on her, but they hadn't. She had no personality, and people paid her no mind unless she acted fashionable and above the riffraff. Why couldn't she be more like her ma? She was sweet and kind and always taking in children who needed a home.

Olga came in and placed her supper on a table in front of the sofa. She didn't wait for Scarlett to thank her, she just turned and left the room.

Scarlett couldn't feel sorry for herself. One day she'd find someone worthy of her friendship. A person who knew what it was to be part of the upper crust of society.

The stew was tasteless to her. It was more of an exercise in chewing. Dillon was bound to be very late in coming home. She'd pretend to be asleep so he wouldn't offer to carry her to her bed. She'd heard whispers about the smell of cheap perfume and lip rouge stains on a cheating man's neck. It was better not to know.

Olga reappeared, took the empty plate, and brought her a cup of coffee. Again, she left without a word. The coffee was welcome, though. It would help to keep her awake.

"I have your nightgown. Seeing as Dillon has plans for the evening we might as well get you changed. You'll have to sleep on the couch, though." Elda said. She put the nightgown down and helped Scarlett undress. After a few moments, she finally slipped the nightgown on.

Scarlett hated when Elda helped her. She never had the courtesy to look away. Scarlett felt disgusted afterward due to Elda's stares. It was unseemly.

When Elda was finished, Scarlett shivered in dislike.

"I wonder if we can hear Angel sing from up here?" Elda murmured.

"I doubt it. I don't hear much from town except if they are building something down there."

Elda went to the window and opened it. "It's so quiet out. Oh wait, I think I can hear her. I can only imagine all the men watching her. Dillon was excited to hear her. She's such a pretty little thing too."

"Little?" Scarlett asked. She didn't care if she sounded annoyed. Elda was the most annoying person she knew.

"She's petite and thin, but she fills out the top of her dress. Her hair is a beautiful shade of blond and she wore it down. It hung down to her thighs."

"You sound as though you admire her. Surely a woman working in a saloon doesn't deserve admiration."

Shrugging, Elda closed the window. "The men certainly appreciate her. Look how dark it is. I bet it's later than we think. Are you done with your coffee? I'd like to get everything cleaned up before I go to bed."

"Yes, I'm done."

Edna took the cup away. A minute later, she came back. "Ma is already asleep. I'm going to join her. Good night."

Scarlett nodded. Her mind felt a bit fuzzy. She must be coming down with something, but what she didn't know. She'd never felt so tired and confused except for earlier. She lay down and pulled the quilt over her. Dillon was sure to come home soon. Maybe he was still listening to that Angel.

Dillon frowned as he rode his horse up to his house. Why was it so dark inside? There was only a dimly lit oil lamp in the kitchen. He hadn't stayed at the saloon very long. He took care of his horse and then headed into the house. It certainly was quiet.

He walked to the kitchen and turned up the lamp. He heard a small cry and started for Scarlett's room, but he spotted her asleep on the sofa with Missy curled up against her. Scarlett's head moved back and forth as though she was having a bad dream. Should he wake her?

He leaned over and touched her shoulder. "Scarlett, wake up." Her lashes fluttered a bit but she didn't wake. He was about to leave her when she cried out and tears flowed down her face. What was she dreaming about? He grabbed the lamp from the kitchen and went to his bedroom. He had to set the lamp on the dresser so he could pull the covers down. After that, he went back and lifted Scarlett into his arms, holding her tight to him. Her body was nice and soft. Usually when he carried her, she was as stiff as a board.

She stirred and whimpered as he lay her down on his bed. After he quickly undressed, he lowered the lamp to a dim glow. He didn't want to put it out, fearing she might wake up scared. She had quieted down and looked so peaceful. Missy, of course, made herself at home on his bed. Quietly, he slipped in under the covers and pulled her into his arms. He kissed her forehead and fell asleep.

THE SUN WAS BEGINNING to rise as Dillon got out of bed and dressed. He stared at his wife and smiled. She looked angelic in her slumber. He wished he could spend the day with her. Maybe if they got to know one another better... He sighed. Why was being kind so easy for him while seeming to be a major struggle for her?

Some coffee before he carried her back to the couch sounded good. He needed to check her leg and ankle. As he left the bedroom, the welcome smell of coffee filled his nose. Upon reaching the kitchen, he found Elda still in her nightgown without anything covering it. He pursed his lips and then gave her a slight smile.

"Good morning, Elda. Thanks for having the coffee ready." He poured himself a cup and escaped into the main room. There was no way he was getting caught with Elda in her indecent clothing. She'd had a small smile pulling at her lips, obviously aware of how see-through her gown was. Well, he wasn't interested.

Elda brought him a plate full of scrambled eggs and bacon. She leaned down far enough to show her breasts. Dillon quickly turned his head away.

"If you need anything else, call me," she said. When he didn't answer, she frowned at him and then disappeared into the kitchen.

What type of woman tried to seduce another woman's husband? He'd lost his appetite, but he needed to eat. It was a long time until the noon meal, and he needed something in his stomach. He'd just finished his meal when he heard Olga scolding her daughter and then sending her to get dressed. He stifled a laugh.

He got up and went into his bedroom to find Scarlett sitting up in his bed, wide-eyed. "Good morning, Scarlett. I hope you slept well."

"How did I get here? I was sleeping on the couch."

"You were restless and crying, so I carried you in here. You quieted down as soon as you were in my arms." Her rosy blush was enchanting.

"You didn't try to take advantage of me, did you?" She folded her arms in front of her and stared at him.

"Of course not. I'm insulted that you'd even think I'd do such a thing. I try to be a moral upstanding man. I didn't even look when Elda was showing herself."

Her mouth opened. "What? What was she showing?"

She wouldn't stop until she got an answer. He took a deep breath. "She had her nightgown on when she made and served breakfast."

Scarlett inhaled sharply. "I knew she had her eye on you. What is she supposed to think when you give her presents? You brought this on yourself."

Whatever she was talking about, he didn't even want to

know. "I'll have Olga help you dress while I saddle my horse. Then I'll carry you to the couch."

"How was Angel? I waited up for you as long as I could but you didn't come home." He didn't like the sour expression she wore.

"Angel is a very talented singer."

"Is singing all she does there?"

Annoyed, he shook his head. "I don't know. I'll be back." He hurried out of the bedroom before he said something he'd be sorry for.

In the barn, he carried the saddle and tack to his horse's stall. He smiled at the tall dark horse. "Coal, be happy you're a bachelor. I have no idea what my wife is talking about." The horse snorted, and Dillon laughed. He led the saddled horse out of the barn and tied the reins to the hitching post outside of the house.

He put a pretend smile on and went inside. He walked toward the bedroom and stopped short when he saw Scarlett trying to cover her nakedness with her hands while Elda was holding Scarlett's shift out of reach. He didn't like the look in Elda's eyes.

Without much thought, he entered the room, told Elda to leave, and handed Scarlett her shift. He turned his back to give her privacy.

"Is Elda always like that?"

"Yes, she makes me very uncomfortable. She seems to find it funny."

"Why don't you ask Olga to help you instead?"

"I've been told if I make trouble, I'd be left to fend for myself."

He heard the tears in her voice and turned toward her. He scooped her up and held her on his lap. "You'll never be left to fend for yourself." He pulled her close and tucked her head under his chin. "You have me."

"Do I? You lived at your shop until my accident. Were you ever planning to come back?" She sounded so fragile.

"Of course I was. I just didn't know how to come and talk to you. I would have asked the pastor, but he's been visiting other towns that don't have a church."

She pulled her head back far enough to look into his eyes. She must have seen something she liked. She then wrapped her arms around his neck and laid her head on his chest. She sighed contently.

Somehow, she made him feel good about himself, like maybe he'd said the right thing for once. "Would you like to spend the day at the shop with me? I can find a comfortable chair and footstool for you."

Keeping her head against his chest, she gave a tiny nod. She felt so soft and womanly. It was a miracle he hadn't made her his wife in truth. Things needed to be right between them, and hopefully today would be the start.

"Here let's get you dressed." He lifted her hand set her on the bed. He stood and reached for a blue dress that was draped over a chair. He looked at it to figure out where the buttons were.

He frowned. The dress was stained. "Did you mean to wear this dress?"

"It's one of my favorites. Why?"

He turned the dress so she could see the stains on it.

She put her hand over her mouth as her eyes grew wide. "It looks to be splattered with grease. I don't know how to properly fry things so I stick to soups and stews. I don't understand."

He shrugged. "Tell me what other dress you want, and I'll get it from your room."

"I have a burgundy one that should work. It has a little jacket with it."

He walked to her room and opened the wardrobe. There

weren't many dresses hung inside of it. She'd had enough trunks with her he'd have thought the wardrobe would be overstuffed. He grabbed a green one with a jacket. The burgundy one wasn't there.

There was bound to be trouble. He tried to smile as he brought the dress to Scarlett.

"I hate to complain but that's green." She smiled. Her smile dimmed as he stood there. "Where is the burgundy one?"

"It wasn't there. Let's get this one on you and I'll carry you over to your room so you can check what else is gone."

Her eyes widened in alarm but she nodded. He helped her into the dress and saw the woolen stockings left on the chair. Certainly he wouldn't be required to put those on her legs… He swallowed hard as he picked them up and turned to Scarlett. "I guess these are next."

She nodded, but as he knelt down, she began to shake her head. "This is, I mean, well go ahead, but don't look."

She seemed more nervous that he was. He decided to just get it over with. He put her uninjured foot onto his leg and he gently put the stocking on her. So far so good. He got it past her ankle and then her calf but when he reached her knee, heat rushed to his face. He went ahead and did it. It was so different from when he'd simply tended her injuries. That had been necessary. This seemed…intimate. He swallowed and finished unrolling the stocking and eased out a breath. One done, one to go.

She laughed.

"What's so funny?"

"You tickled my thighs is all. Listen, it's no big deal. You are my husband. Now the foot, you need to be extra gentle with. Elda wasn't the gentlest."

He frowned. "I shouldn't have left you in her care."

"You didn't know." Her soft voice soothed him somewhat.

"I'm going to pull up your skirts to take a look at your leg. Did Olga tend to wound?"

Scarlett bit her lip and shook her head. "No. But it doesn't hurt more than it did."

He shifted her skirts to show her injured leg. "The bandage is filthy." Gently he removed it and then set back on his heels. It was ringed in red with tiny striations starting on her skin.

"Olga! Get in here!"

"Dillon, what is it?" Scarlett asked. She began to shake. "There's something wrong isn't there?"

Before he had a chance to answer, Olga was there.

"Can I get something for you?"

"Get over here and take a look at her leg." He didn't care how sharp his voice was.

Olga put her hand over her heart. "Oh my. I thought Elda was taking care of it. Dillon, it's unseemly for you to be where you are with her skirts up."

"I don't care what you think. This is my wife! Elda get in here!" His voice was louder than he intended.

Elda gasped when she entered the room. "What's going on? Are we to witness your coupling?"

Dillon shook his head in disgust. "Come here and look at her wound. Now!"

Elda hurried over and stared at Scarlett's leg. "I'll wash it."

"Boil some water and put a sharp knife in it to sterilize it. But first, I need hot water and a clean cloth. Fetch my whiskey for me."

Olga stared at him. "Surely you don't want to drink spirits this early."

"It's for Scarlett. I need to disinfect her leg." Both women stared at him. "Go! Now!" It gave him a bit of satisfaction when they scurried out of the bedroom.

He glanced up at Scarlett, dismayed by her tears.

"Are you going to have to cut my leg off?"

Taking her hand in his, he kissed her palm. "No, but I need to cut away some of this infected skin. It's going to hurt. Do you know where they keep the laudanum?"

"In my room on the table next to my bed."

He gave her hand a quick squeeze then rose and went to get the medicine. For a few moments, he stood in Scarlett's room trying to let his anger go. He'd need a steady hand to help her. He was angry at Olga and Elda, but most of all himself. He should have made sure his wife was healing properly.

He went to the bedside table and grabbed the bottle of laudanum, frowning at its weight. It felt very light. He shook it and then opened the dark glass bottle. There wasn't much left. Scarlett should have told him the pain was unbearable. He ran his fingers through his hair as he tried once again to let go of his anger. He was a poor excuse for a husband. He'd just have to do better.

MORTIFIED WAS the only word that came to mind as she lay there with her skirts up high on her thighs. Scarlett wanted to hide away from it all. Olga and Elda were useless, and Dillon seemed furious. Her leg had hurt but she didn't think it was becoming infected. Tears pricked at the back of her eyes. She felt a bit lightheaded and very confused. What had happened to her burgundy dress? Why was the one Elda left for her to wear stained?

It was her own fault. Perhaps she did need to be nicer. But what if she was nice and people still didn't like her? After all, what was there to like? The parents she had been born to had never paid her any mind. She hadn't been good enough for them to want to spend time with. Then they went to heaven without her.

Elda brought in the hot water and a cloth. "Well look at you with your skirts up. I always thought you were a light skirt." She chuckled. "I bet it'll hurt something awful. I'm glad it's not me."

"Elda, that's enough." Dillon said sternly. "Please leave us until I ask for the knife. I want to talk to my wife."

Elda's expression turned sour before she turned and walked away.

"Dillon?"

"Scarlett, why didn't you tell me you're in so much pain? It must hurt dreadfully. Most of your laudanum is gone." He actually sounded concerned.

"It hurts, but I haven't been taking laudanum after the first three days. Only when you came home at night. I was afraid of hurting my ankle more if it didn't pain me. I was afraid I'd forget it was sprained and try to walk on it. It gave me a headache."

His brow furrowed.

"What's wrong?"

Dillon pulled a chair up to the bed and looked her leg over again. He dipped the cloth into the steaming water and then set the cloth on the wound.

"Ouch," Scarlett balled her hands in the bed covers and tried to stay still. Her body began to shake.

"I know it hurts, love. I'm sorry. I should have checked your leg daily. I could have avoided all this pain for you."

He took the cloth off, rinsed it in the water, and set it on her leg again.

She could hardly catch her breath. "The pain is going to get worse before it gets better, isn't it?"

"I'm afraid so. Are you sure about the laudanum? I wouldn't judge you if you'd used it all."

"I didn't."

He nodded. "I believe you."

Olga came in and handed him a bottle of whiskey and a glass. He didn't bother to thank her, and she quickly left.

"Don't go far. I'm going to need someone to hold her down in a bit," he yelled loud enough to be probably heard throughout the house. He splashed a bit of the dark amber liquid into a glass and put it on the table. Then he put a pillow under Scarlett's head and handed her the glass. "Drink it down. It'll help with the pain."

She didn't like the strong smell, and she wasn't going to like the taste either, but she did as he bade and took a sip. "Oh! What are you trying to do to me? People willingly drink this?"

His lips twitched as though he was going to smile, but the smile never appeared. "It helps to swig it all down at once."

She doubted it, but she drank it all down. It took all her concentration to keep it from coming back up. She groaned out loud when he poured more into the glass and handed it to her. "I don't—I can't—"

"Yes you can. There isn't enough laudanum to take any pain away. Please? I can't bear to know I'll hurt you." He stared into her eyes, and she nodded.

The second glass was as bad as the first, but it made her feel warm inside. She winced as he once again rinsed the cloth and reapplied it.

"I don't think we'll go to town today. Lou or Homer will be along to see where I am soon. They can handle the small things."

She nodded and frowned when he gave her yet another bit of whiskey to drink. This time she downed it as fast as she could. Her body began to relax.

"How are you feeling?"

She smiled. "Quite unlike myself. Do what you have to, I'll survive."

Giving her a nod, he took the cloth and doused it in whiskey then held it down on her leg.

It burned so bad she tried to move out of his reach but he was so strong. Tears poured down her face as she cried out.

Both Olga and Elda stood in the doorway. Olga stepped forward and handed Dillon the knife.

He took it without looking at either of the women. "This is going to hurt."

Scarlett swallowed hard and nodded.

"Olga, I need you to hold her down."

"I don't think I'm strong enough," she replied coolly.

Dillon shook his head. "Then I need you both to help. Olga, hold down her shoulders. Elda, I need you to hold her leg still." He waited until the women were in position.

Scarlett began to tremble, and beads of sweat formed on her forehead. She closed her eyes and made her hands into fists as she waited. The skin around the gash was already sore to begin with. She didn't want to scream, but it would be impossible not to. Holding her breath, she waited for Dillon to start. Clenching her teeth, she tried to think of her parents and their ranch. But as soon as the first cut was made, the only thing she could think about was the pain. She screamed and she screamed loud.

Try as she might, she couldn't move away. It seemed to go on forever. Surely, the gash wasn't that long. Her breathing became labored and she hated both Olga and Elda for their lack of care. Why didn't she just pass out like she'd seen others do?

"I'm almost done, Scarlett. You're doing really well. Hold on for just a bit more." Dillon's vice soothed her a bit. Nodding, she bit her lip and ended up making it bleed as he finished.

He wiped the sweat off her forehead and then staunched the bleeding on her lip. "You were so brave. The most hardened of cowboys couldn't have done better."

She barely nodded. Turning her head, she glared at both Olga and Elda until they both appeared ashamed and glanced away from her.

"You can let her go now. Elda, Scarlett seems to be missing several of her dresses. I'd like them returned in their original condition before the day is out."

Scarlett warmed at his words. He was taking her side.

He leaned down and kissed her forehead. "I'm going to let you rest, then I'll send one of the boys to get some laudanum before I stitch you up."

Scarlett gulped. "It's going to leave a scar isn't it?"

He leaned down and whispered into her ear. "Love, no one will ever see it but me."

He smiled as her face flamed. "Rest." His expression hardened as he ushered the other two women out of the room.

Scarlett allowed her tears to flow. She'd thought it was all done, but there were still stitches to get through. What had happened to all the laudanum? Perhaps Olga had an addiction to it. She'd heard of such things. Her head felt a bit woozy. She never wanted to drink that nasty whiskey again.

CHAPTER SEVEN

What a draining day! Working in the smithy was hard work but taking care of Scarlett's leg was downright draining. It was different doctoring someone you cared about. Dillon sank back in a chair that he placed near Scarlett.

He'd expected hysterics from her but all in all, she'd been a trooper. She'd handled herself better than a lot of men he knew. She was not at all the spoiled little girl he'd believed her to be. What kind of person she was, he really didn't know.

He decided to have Lou find a sofa to put in the corner of the smithy for Scarlett. He didn't trust anyone else to take care of her. It was his fault Scarlett's leg had gotten infected. He'd take better care of her from now on.

He stared down on her as she slept and smiled. Tenderness filled him and caring, a lot of caring. Last week he'd decided to build his own house, but now he knew he'd never do it. Missy jumped up on Scarlett, stretched, circled a few times, and finally settled on top of her. She was a cute cat he supposed.

He wasn't about to leave Scarlett in the living room to spend the night, so he gently moved Missy and then lifted Scarlett into his arms. He held her close, and her eyelashes fluttered for a moment, but she fell back to sleep. He started for her room but turned into his instead and lay her down on the bed, making sure she was comfortable. He fanned out her glorious hair on the pillow and smiled at the effect. She almost looked angelic.

He left her to make sure all the doors were locked. Tomorrow he'd give Olga and Elda the boot. Their services were no longer required…or wanted. Imagine taking Scarlett's dresses and leaving her with a stained one to put on. He shook his head. Sometimes a person just never knew what other people were capable of.

Finally he closed the door to his bedroom, undressed down to his underwear and got into bed beside his wife. He longed to hold her in his arms, but he wasn't sure his attention would be welcome. He'd left her alone too long. What he should have done was talked to her and gotten everything straightened out between them.

He'd make up for it.

THE NEXT MORNING he woke before Scarlett and told Olga and Elda to leave. They both told him he was an ungrateful dolt. And they were appalled by his treatment of them. He didn't care. In fact, closing the door behind them when they left gave him a bit of relief. Although they were bound to badmouth both him and Scarlett.

He made eggs with toast and then went to wake Scarlett. She was trying to stand on one foot. Shaking his head, he swept her up into his arms and carried her to the table.

"Eat your breakfast. It'll be a long day at the smithy. You might want to bring one of your books."

"Elda said you actually bought those books for her and I was just borrowing them. When I asked to read Ivanhoe, she told me she'd taken it home."

His eyes widened. "You believed her?"

She stared at the floor. "Yes, I did."

He wanted to growl but he didn't. "I'll get your books back. And your dresses too. Don't you worry."

They ate breakfast, and then he helped her to dress. It wasn't as awkward this time, she didn't seem as frightened. Afterward, he went outside and hitched the horses to the wagon. There'd be a lot of talk in town with Scarlett at the smithy. He hoped they all knew better than to say anything derogatory about his wife.

He went back into the house, grabbed her cape, and lifted her. She smiled, but her lips trembled slightly.

"It'll be just fine. I'll be there, and you like Homer and Lou."

She nodded as he lifted her onto the wagon. She settled herself, but she couldn't hide her shaking hands.

She wasn't the cold, uncaring woman she usually portrayed. He had a lot to learn about his wife, but it would have to be on her own terms. He didn't want her to place more distance between them. He drove the horses slowly so not to jostle her, and finally they arrived.

"Here we are." He set the brake and tied off the lines. Then he jumped down and held up his arms for her to lean his way. He scooped her up and carried her into his shop.

He was getting there a bit later than usual, and the shop was filled with customers as well as the regulars who hung around. The sofa looked inviting with a pretty quilt and matching pillow on it. After setting her down, he placed the quilt over her and made sure she was comfortable. With all the attention, a bright crimson painted her face.

"Most of you know, Scarlett, my beautiful wife. She is

going to finish recovering here during the day. So watch your language." This time he didn't hear a grumble.

Homer came with a big list of things to repair and make. Several horses needed shoeing too.

"I'll start on the bigger things while you two work the bellows, and then Homer, I'll need you to repair what you can while Lou acts as farrier." Both apprentices looked proud to be asked to work on their own. It was probably time to raise their wages.

Dillon jumped right in and began to make a tripod for the Lynches to use for cooking over the fire. It wasn't hard, but it had a few tricky spots. The bellows got going, and the fire grew hot enough to start.

SCARLETT WATCHED the men coming and going, but most of all she watched Dillon. He drew her gaze time and again. He was a brawny man filled with confidence. His shirt pulled tight across his back as he worked, and his muscles rippled. When he pounded on the metal at the anvil, she could see his biceps bulge. He was certainly strong, but watching him had never affected her before. Even as his shirt grew damp with perspiration, it didn't take away from his allure. Why now? She'd always thought him handsome, but this was something more. Her stomach felt fluttery, and she swore her heart skipped a beat whenever he looked up and caught her gaze.

Lunch time came and with it came Lolly. She stopped short of the smithy and stared at Scarlett. Then she turned a questioning gaze at Dillon. Scarlett glanced away. Lolly wasn't a threat, and she needn't treat her that way.

Dillon wiped his hands on his trousers and approached Lolly. "Oh, good. I was just getting hungry. As you can see, my wife is here. I wanted to be sure she heals properly."

Lolly nodded her head at Scarlett, who nodded back. The look of defeat on Lolly's face almost saddened Scarlett. She looked down at the quilt and traced the pattern with her finger. When had she decided to be kind to husband stealers? Something must have changed, but Scarlett wasn't sure what.

Dillon placed a slice of meatloaf, a piece of cornbread, and some green beans on a fresh piece of wood as though it was a tray and set it on Scarlett's lap. "Would you like coffee or water?"

There was something in the way he looked at her but she didn't have a clue what it meant. "Coffee is just fine, thank you."

He pulled a chair up right next to her and set the tray of food on his lap while Homer brought over their coffee.

"Thanks, Homer," Dillon said.

It was the nicest lunch she could remember. There wasn't any fine crystal or servants, but she didn't need anyone besides Dillon. Had she been dropped on her head? "I have gaps in my memory from this last week. Did something happen to me during that time?"

Dillon finished chewing before he answered. "Not that I'm aware of. I didn't know you had memory problems."

"There were a few times I could have sworn I was in a different place when I woke up."

Dillon frowned. "Like what?"

"I remember sitting in a chair looking out over the town but waking up in my bed. Then there was a time I'd been on the sofa but ended up in your bed." She furrowed her brow. "It was very confusing."

"The laudanum."

She tilted her head. "What do you mean?"

"That's where it all went. I bet they were dosing you with it. It would make sense."

Her mouth dropped open. "Why? I don't understand. It wasn't as though I could get up and go anywhere."

He stared at her for a bit then shrugged his shoulders. "I can't think of any reason."

"At least I now know I'm not going crazy." She smiled at him and his returning smile warmed her heart. She sat there long after the trays were gone and Dillon had gone back to work wondering about the new feelings she was experiencing. It wasn't just that he was handsome or strong. It went beyond that, and it was puzzling. Was this what her mother felt for her father? It couldn't be. Their love was there in the open for all to see. Perhaps it was the beginning of really liking him?

She stole another glance at him. Everyone seemed to like him. All day people had come in to chat. He was kind and patient. She would have told a few of his customers to go somewhere else but in the end, he always charmed them.

At the moment, he was fixing and sharpening a plow for a farmer. He sure was a busy man. No wonder he was never home before dark.

As she listened to the men talk, she was happy to hear that Matilda's rash had cleared up. Now, they mostly talked about what was best to plant and when. Despite all the noise, she felt her eyes beginning to close but then she heard a woman's voice, and Scarlett came wide awake.

The woman was very lovely. Her features were dainty, and her blond hair hung all the way down her back. She nodded to all the men who greeted her, but her eyes lit up when she saw Dillon.

Scarlett's stomach clenched, and her heart squeezed. She knew who it was before Dillon made the introductions. It was Angel, the woman from the saloon with the heavenly voice. Dillon's speech was unnaturally soft as he introduced them. He smiled kindly, and Angel returned it with a lovely smile of her own.

"It's so good to finally meet you, Scarlett. Dillon has told me much about you."

Scarlett cocked her brow and lifted her chin. "Oh, did he?" How dare she, a soiled dove, call her by her first name? The woman didn't know her place. Scarlett gave her a cold smile meant to warn Angel away.

All eyes were on the two of them, and Scarlett was livid. "Come here often to see my husband?" She gave Angel her best glare, but Angel didn't seem to care.

"Why yes, he's the nicest man I know."

All the men in the shop began whispering to each other. Something dodgy was going on and Scarlett swore to get to the bottom of it. All of her good feelings left her, and she was filled with doubt and anger. She should have known what she had felt was fleeting at best. What a fool she was. She'd actually thought she was falling for her husband. Her heart hurt. She thought he was falling for her too. Her shoulders dropped as she turned away. It just wasn't worth it. It wasn't worth the pain or the jealousy. She'd been nothing but a fool.

She feigned great interest in the quilted pattern once again. If Dillon would rather be with that strumpet, so be it. Too bad she was stuck in the smithy for the day. Pretending to sleep might be the best course of action. She sighed and made herself comfortable on the sofa, closing her eyes while listening.

"Will you be at the saloon again tonight?" Angel asked.

"I have my wife to take care of," Dillon answered.

"You found someone to take care of her before so you could come and see me sing. Am I not allowed in here anymore?" Scarlett could hear the pouting in Angel's voice.

"Everyone is allowed in here," Dillon answered. Gracious, how very casual he sounded.

"Good! I think I'll just pull up a stool and watch you work."

The nerve of that hussy! Just who did she think she was? Scarlett closed her eyes tighter. Any reaction from her would be fodder for gossip, and frankly, she couldn't afford to be talked about anymore. It was proving to be a long and exhausting day. She listened for a while but just heard the pounding of the metal. At long last, she drifted off.

She felt something on her face and she quickly sat up. It was Dillon caressing her cheek. "Oh, you scared me."

"I'm glad you were able to get some rest. I was just about to go to the store to get more medicine for you. Did you need anything else?"

His eyes were so full of concern she almost forgot about Angel. "No more medicine, please. It makes me so woozy."

He sat down on the sofa next to her and took her small hand in his big strong one. "I was going to find something to put on the gash."

"I could use a needle and thread. I have a feeling I have a few dresses to repair. Do you think you could get a couple yards of lace? If it's too expensive don't worry about it." She suddenly felt shy under his intense gaze.

His lips twitched. "I might be able to afford a piece or two. I'll be back. I have your books to collect from Elda too. I feel bad that I hadn't noticed how they were treating you."

She smiled. "I didn't even know until the last. It's not your fault."

Leaning over, he gave her a quick kiss on her cheek before he stood and left.

Upon looking around, she was surprised to see Angel and a few more saloon girls all sitting on stools talking to the men. What would their wives have to say? She'd bet they didn't know, yet. Not from her though. There were many other women who would be willing to spill the beans. As she watched them, she noticed that one had her eye on Homer and another watched Lou. Scarlett's breath caught. Lou was too young to consort with that type of woman.

She intentionally caught the woman's eye and gave her a glare. The woman must have known she was doing wrong because she blushed. It was doubtful much made her blush anymore. That soiled dove had some nerve.

Most of the men in there stared at Angel. She smiled sweetly at each of them, but Scarlett saw the slight annoyance in her. She was here for Dillon and no one else. Too bad Dillon was going to be busy for the next few weeks. It was downright sinful to try to catch the fancy of a married man.

When Dillon finally returned, his arms were laden with packages. He awkwardly handed her the two books and then went through the back and put the purchases in the wagon. He came back in with one package in his hand and sat next to her.

"She put up a fuss but I got most of your dresses back for you. Guess what she was wearing?"

"My burgundy dress?"

"The very one. I pretended not to notice. Good riddance, I say." He gave her a heart-stopping grin.

That had been one of her best dresses, but she couldn't help but grin back. "You're right of course."

He handed her the brown paper wrapped package.

She smiled with excitement. After she untied the string around it, she pulled back the paper. She immediately fingered the different types of fine lace in awe. She hadn't known what to expect but nothing this nice. "It's beautiful! How many did you buy? It looks very expensive."

"One is French, another is Irish. I don't know what the others are. Mrs. Blains ordered them and they never sold, so her husband gave me a deal I couldn't refuse. He wanted it out of his store. Good fortune, I'd say." His smile reached his eyes as he met her gaze and held it.

The intimate moment didn't last long, as Angel oohed and ahhed over the lace. Scarlett quickly rewrapped the package and held it to her chest.

"I have a few things to finish up. Can you stand to be here just a little longer?"

"Of course." She nodded.

"Good." He put his apron on and went back to heating and shaping the metal.

As he returned to work, leaving her cuddling his gift to her chest, Dillon realized that Scarlett's happiness was his happiness. Her joy in something so small as lace delighted him. She didn't like that the saloon ladies were in the shop, but he wasn't about to tell anyone they weren't welcome.

He finished his work, took off his apron, washed his hands and face, and then asked Lou to harness the horses for him. Walking over to the sofa, he smiled at his wife. "It was nice having you here with me today. I'll get you home so we can feed that mangy cat of yours."

"Mangy?"

He laughed. "I suppose mangy isn't the best word. Stray is a better word."

"She's no longer a stray. She has a home with you and me."

A warm feeling flowed through him. It sounded to him that she was planning on staying. Now he needed to court her in some fashion. The lace had been a good first step. He leaned down and gathered her close as he carried her to the wagon. Her face had turned a delightful shade of red as she wrapped her arms around his neck. His heart began to beat faster as he realized she hadn't tensed up, and he found himself desiring her. Too bad she wasn't in any condition or ready for them to be together. Gently he set her up on the wagon bench and then tucked a blanket around her.

"I'll have you home soon." He climbed up and grabbed the reins, and they rode up to their house. Dillon jumped down and carried her inside. He almost tripped over Missy, and he grumbled good-naturedly about the mangy cat.

"I heard that!" Her voice was teasing, and he stared into her eyes. They sparkled as they had never before. Things were looking up.

"I'll set you down on the sofa then I'll make us something to eat. I don't even know what we have stocked in the kitchen." He set her down slowly and carefully, prolonging the contact with her soft warm body.

"I wish I could help. I'm a fair cook, you know, except for frying some things. My mother made sure we knew how to do anything on a ranch, including work considered a man's job. She never wanted us to be put in a position that we had to rely on a man not of our choosing."

"A wise woman to be sure. Do you consider me to be a man of your choosing?" He held his breath. He shouldn't have asked if he didn't want to know the answer. She'd chosen him sight unseen, and she hadn't taken an instant liking to him.

Her lips twitched. "You'll do." She stared into his eyes and he could feel her changing opinion of him. He felt her smile all the way into his heart. It startled him. He'd escorted young ladies before, but no one ever had this effect on him.

"I'll be back. Would you like some water?"

"I'll be fine. I'm hungry is all." Missy jumped up on her stomach and circled a few times until she found a comfortable spot before she lay down.

He walked into the kitchen and whistled as he made eggs, bacon, and biscuits. He flipped the last strip of bacon then abruptly stopped. When was the last time he'd whistled? His heart felt lighter today. Things were changing for the better, and he hoped it continued on the same path.

They ate together on the sofa and talked about their lives before they knew each other. She'd had a hard life filled with doubt, disappointment and sadness until she was adopted by Lynn and Smitty. He was tempted to ask about her wedding that never happened but decided not to. That other man's loss was his gain.

He wiped his mouth with his napkin. "I don't have anything for dessert I'm afraid."

"That's fine. I'm full. You cook very well."

"I've had to cook for myself when I'm home."

"Why didn't you just hire someone?"

He took a deep breath. It wouldn't do to get into this argument again. "I like my privacy. I have people around me all day long, and when I come home I want to be able to relax without someone wanting to wait on me."

She nodded. "I guess I assumed that with a house so big you'd have to have someone to clean it. I also thought that might be the reason you took a wife. I misjudged you, and I'm sorry." She appeared very contrite.

It was probably hard for her to apologize. She seemed unpracticed doing it. But she did it.

"I had big dreams of having a large family. As each new bedroom was built, I imagined a son or daughter sleeping in it. I just wanted what I never had. I was an apprentice to a very kind man, named Charlie. I learned just about everything I know from him. He died and I was going to take over his smithy, but then I heard about the beauty of Silver Falls. I still need to take you to see them. Its exquisiteness is incomparable. Anyway, I like being part of building a new town and getting to know everyone. I know having everyone in the smithy is a bit chaotic but I enjoy it, and I'm not going to ban the women from the saloon. I like it to be known as a place where all are welcome."

She nodded. "No wonder they want you to be the mayor. You're a good, kind man."

The earth seemed to stand still at her words. Dillon leaned over and cradled her cheek in his big hand. He turned her head and brought his head down close to hers. He needed to taste her sweet lips, but he was nervous at the same time. He lifted his gaze, and discovered anticipation burning in her eyes. But he pulled back at the last minute. Nice and slow was the way to go.

Disappointment flashed across her face.

"Tell me about Dexter," he found himself asking. Despite his resolve, he didn't seem able to let it go. "Did you love him?"

Her eyes widened. "I'm not sure I even knew what love was. He was the most eligible bachelor in town, and it was like winning a prize. He never kissed me, and he only held my hand once." She glanced down at her hands. "I don't know why he proposed." She shook her head. "Yes I do. We went on a picnic and while he napped, I loosened the wheel on the carriage. We were stuck there after dark, and his father made him propose. I'm ashamed of my actions now. Of course, I never told anyone why he proposed. I acted like Queen Victoria of England, thinking I was so much better than the rest of the town, including the few friends I had. When he jilted me I was more embarrassed than heartbroken." She sighed and peered at him. "I don't know why I'm such a horrible person. You're the first person I've been truly sorry for acting like a…a…"

"Spoiled brat?"

Tears filled her eyes. "Yes, like a spoiled brat." She quickly turned her head. Her shoulders shook as she cried silently. Dillon figured she did a lot of silent crying. It was a big step for her to admit she was wrong.

He stood and gathered up the dirty dishes. "I need to get these done." She didn't look at him.

CHAPTER EIGHT

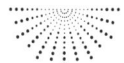

He hated her. Why wouldn't he? She'd told him just how awful a person she was, and he'd walked away. It didn't surprise her, but it hurt beyond anything she'd felt before. She had thought they were making strides toward each other, but they were probably further apart than when they began. It wasn't his fault he didn't want to be stuck with her. Why did she have to sprain her ankle? She couldn't just up and leave. She'd bide her time and when she was healed she'd go, and leave him in the peace he deserved.

It was just his bad luck of the draw that he'd ended up with her. She swallowed hard. The pain in her heart might just crush her. She'd have to be brave and let him go. If Angel was the woman he'd rather have… She cried harder and then she got hold of herself and put on the blank face she used to hide all of her feelings. She'd been so horrible to so many people, she wasn't sure she knew how to be nice, truly nice to anyone anymore. Going back home wasn't the best option. Everyone would be disappointed in her plus she had no friends.

There was no use feeling sorry for herself. She had done this. She had behaved terribly, and she had no excuses. What a fool she was. It was too late now for her and Dillon, and she wasn't sure what to do. She couldn't let him catch wind of her plan. Her ankle would be fine in a few days, and she'd be left alone in this big house again.

Dillon came from the kitchen and carried her to her own room. He unbuttoned her dress for her and handed over her nightgown and then left without a word. She sat on the bed feeling as though she was dying inside. It was too much of a struggle for her to get undressed so she lay down on the bed in her dress and waited for sleep to come. Unfortunately, it didn't.

When morning light filtered through the window, her door opened and Dillon walked in. His hair was disheveled and he had circles under his eyes. It seemed he hadn't gotten any sleep either, and that was her fault. She was poison.

"You didn't put your nightgown on."

"No."

He didn't ask why. He just pulled another dress out from the wardrobe and handed it to her. He sat behind her and helped to get her undressed. He wasn't as slow and gentle as he'd been before but she understood. He then helped her to dress. As soon as he was done, he left the room.

Her heart shattered. He really didn't want anything to do with her. She grabbed her hairbrush and brushed her hair until it gleamed. She then put it up using her hair pins. He hadn't brought her water to wash with. Even Missy looked miserable.

He brought her to the smithy without so much as a word and then he set her on the sofa. This time she had her book with her. She tried to read, but her thoughts kept drifting to Dillon. She couldn't keep her gaze from following his every move. He did something to her insides. She felt as though butterflies were flying in her stomach. Her heart skipped a beat if he happened to meet her gaze, but he never looked at her for long. She was enthralled with him. The way he tilted his head a tiny bit as he sketched out a plan for something he was going to make was endearing. He rolled up his sleeves, and the hair on his arms seemed so masculine. His grin was worth trying to win.

Sadly, she wasn't on the receiving end of his grins. Even Lolly's eyes narrowed at her as though she knew that Scarlett was out of Dillon's good graces. Lolly was oh, so sweet to him, and she received a few grins from him. Scarlett's heart sank.

Somewhere along the line, her heart had become entangled with him. But he wasn't a prize to win. He was the man she cared deeply for, and she had never known she was capable of such strong feelings.

He handed her a makeshift tray of food and then walked over to sit with his friends. It was embarrassing and insulting. Heat flooded her face, and she glanced away. She could feel the gaze of everyone in the shop on her. Her heart dropped, and the pain was unbearable.

Whether they stayed together wasn't her decision. She'd never been in control at all. Now that her feelings had become involved, it was his decision and he seemed inclined to ignore her. Why couldn't she get anything right? She'd always known she was unlovable, but she'd hoped for love anyway. She took a deep breath, pushed the food away, and pretended to read Ivanhoe.

Dillon came and took her tray. He cocked a brow at her but she couldn't meet his gaze. It was too embarrassing. Everyone probably already knew how he felt. She wished she was younger and could run to her pa just to feel his comforting arms around her. But she wasn't a girl anymore; she was a shunned wife.

As she moved her ankle back and forth, she could feel it was stronger. Perhaps if she had a walking stick she could make it back to the house. He deserved better than her and it seemed as though he finally realized it.

There were folded papers on the table near the sofa. She reached for them and carefully unfolded them. She had to hold in the gasp that tried to escape. It was plans for another house and it appeared as though it was going to be right next to where she lived. In the bottom left corner *Dillon's New Home* was written in pencil. A lump formed in her throat as she folded the plans back up. He'd never meant for them to live together.

Her stomach grew queasy, and tears pricked at the backs of her eyes. She didn't have a single friend she could confide in. She'd never been any good at making friends. Staring down at her book, she tried not to cry. It wouldn't be seemly.

"Are you feeling all right? You look a bit pale," Dillon called out to her from the other side of the shop.

She didn't look at him. She just nodded, taking slow, deep breaths all the while. She'd become the town joke.

It wasn't long before a frantic farmer rushed in begging Dillon to come to his farm to fix his plow. Dillon sighed and then nodded. Grabbing his hat and tools, he gave Homer instructions and left without saying a word to her. It was the last straw. There was only so much humiliation a person could take.

She waited until Homer and Lou were busy before she grabbed what would serve as a walking stick and left. It would be too taxing to go up the hill, so she headed for the falls. Maybe the sound of the rushing water would soothe her. The pain was much worse than she imagined but she couldn't go back. She walked until she ran out of boardwalk and then carefully stepped down into the dirt.

Why hadn't he just married one of the women in town?

He had many who would have been delighted. But he'd wanted to do her father a favor. Some favor.

The tall trees swayed in the wind, and the birds chattered noisily. She walked along the path to the falls that she'd seen before until she came to the small clearing. She sat for a bit and admired the sheer beauty of her surroundings. Restless, she stood up again and decided to go on to the next falls. The pain in her heart was more than the pain in her ankle. She needed to get farther away. Much farther.

Her mind whirled as she walked. She heard laughter up ahead and almost turned back, but her curiosity won out. It was the girls from the saloon, bathing and having fun under the next waterfall. What was it like to laugh with such abandon?

She decided to sit on a rock not too far away. She could catch glimpses of the women as she listened to them.

"Oh you're so lucky, Angel. He is such a handsome man," a brunette said.

"He's a brawny one and well-built if you know what I mean." Everyone laughed at Angel's response.

She drew in a quick breath. Who were they talking about? She hoped it was another man. It *had* to be another man.

"Dillon is such a sweetheart. You got the prize of the town, Angel."

"It's a shame he's married, but it's not a real marriage. There are always challenges, but it's not like I'm sharing him with his wife. He mentioned he was building a house for himself," Angel bragged.

"His wife is pretty enough," the brunette commented.

"Aye, she is but he can't stand her. A mail order bride, he said. They don't all end with happy marriages. I think I can be with him, and as soon as she leaves, we can make it official."

"Angel, I think you're dreaming. He'll still be married."

"That is a problem isn't it?" Angel sighed. "We'd best get back to the saloon."

Scarlett listened to them splash each other for a moment before they all scurried out of the water. She hadn't found the peace and quiet she'd searched for. What she'd overheard was too upsetting. She hadn't thought that Dillon was stepping out on her. But apparently he was.

She'd held back her feelings as long as she could, and now she burst into tears. She put her fist in her mouth to mute her sobs. Her shoulders shook violently, and she didn't think she'd ever stop. There were too many emotions in her. So many dreams that had died and all of her hopes were dashed. She couldn't go back to Dillon. She just couldn't.

She got up and walked to the falls. This one was higher than the last. What a beautiful sight, but it didn't help her mood much. She looked to the side of the falls and saw a cabin deep in the woods. Did anyone live there? Did she dare find out? It was either that or go back to Dillon, and she knew her heart wouldn't be able to handle seeing him right now.

DILLON FURROWED HIS BROW. "What do mean she's gone? Gone where? When did she leave?" He tried to rein in his temper. It wouldn't help anyone if he gave in to his anger.

Homer and Lou both appeared a bit pale. "I didn't see her leave," Homer said.

"I didn't notice either, boss," Lou admitted worriedly. "You don't think she walked home, do you?"

Dillon rubbed the back of his neck. "She'd never make it up the hill. She has to be around here somewhere. I'm going to the general store. She might have walked that far."

He doubted she'd go to the store since she hated the

Bains, but it was worth a try. He opened the door and the familiar bell rang. Melly smiled widely as she rushed to his side.

"What can I help you with?" she asked eagerly.

"Have you seen Scarlett? She left the smithy."

"No, but I say good riddance. You didn't even like her. Everyone knows it. Angel told us all about the other house you're building. I'm only sorry you actually married Scarlett. I had hoped…well, you know." She shrugged. "But you have to admit she's not for you."

He frowned. "I wasn't aware you'd spent any time with her."

"I wouldn't have been caught speaking with the likes of her. She even had the nerve to accuse Elda of stealing from her. She's nothing but an opportunist and a liar. Everyone thinks so." Melly's smirk sickened him.

"She didn't lie. I have to go." He left before Melly could say another word. This was his fault. He never should have left the house after the first fight. Now people thought badly of Scarlett.

He walked both sides of the street asking after her, but no one had seen her. Finally, he decided to walk to the falls. She'd wanted to see them, and he had never found the time to take her. He never found the time for her at all, it seemed, not in any way that counted, at least. Heck, what did he know about marriage anyway? His parents had hated each other and spent their lives fighting. Would he and Scarlett ever be able to find their way?

He walked the path to the first waterfall and was disappointed and concerned when he didn't find his wife. He sat on a rock and stared at the ground. What now? When he spotted the imprint from a walking stick, he sighed in relief. She was around here somewhere. With renewed vigor, he stood and followed the tracks.

At last, he saw her up ahead. Her shoulders were shaking and her sobs were heart-wrenching. Why had he been so cold to her after she told him the truth about Dexter? All he wanted from her was the truth and he punished her for giving it. He was an idiot. Everyone made mistakes, and truthfully he could see a change in her, a good change.

Did his reaction to her echo what he'd seen his father do? He walked faster until he got to where she sat weeping, and without a word, he knelt in front of her. She turned her head away but not before he saw how red her eyes had become.

Taking both her hands in his, he quickly asked God for help. Dillon had learned from his mistakes and he wanted a second chance. Then he remembered God's word. *Love is patient and kind; love does not envy or boast; it is not arrogant or rude. It does not insist on its own way; it is not irritable or resentful; it does not rejoice at wrongdoing, but rejoices with the truth. Love bears all things, believes all things, hopes all things, endures all things.*

Dillon felt a glowing warmth take hold inside him. He did love Scarlett. He should not live by his parent's example but by the word of God. They could build a good, strong marriage. If they worked at it and gave each other a second chance... He was blessed to have a second chance, and he wasn't going to waste it.

"Scarlett, look at me." He waited but she didn't turn her head. "Please, Scarlett, I need to apologize, and I hope you can forgive me. I've been so wrong, so very wrong, and I need to put things to right. You told me the truth last night, and I behaved like a jack... I behaved rather badly. I hope that we will always be truthful with each other and try to understand each other."

She still refused to look at him. He sighed. Now what?

"Oh Dillon, give it up." She spoke softly, sadness coloring each word. "You want nothing to do with me, and the whole town knows it. I bet the whole town would cheer the moment I left. Kindness is something you give to everyone else. Warmth is something you bestow to strangers and love is reserved for blondes who sing like angels. There is nothing left for me except contempt and pity. I know I'm no prize, but I dreamed of something more from a marriage. I suppose I'm lucky you don't beat me. But sometimes being ignored or treated coldly can be just as bad. I don't know what to do, but you and I are over. The worst part is, I really thought we could make a go at it. I'd hoped for happiness and children. Now I'll have neither." She raised her head and gave him a long look. "I think we can agree that I don't need to live here any longer. I'd rather go home as a failure than live here while you and Angel build your house next to the one you expect me to live in."

She stood and took a few steps back toward town, but then she stopped and turned back, strain lining her face. "Are you planning on having children with her? I suppose once I'm gone it won't make a difference. Tell people I died or something. It really doesn't matter. I'll have to be content helping my mother take care of the orphans. I'd appreciate it if you took care of the traveling plans for me. I'm penniless." Her voice broke as she spoke.

He stood there in shock. How had it come to this? There would be no talking to her until she calmed herself. He did know one thing, though. There was no way he was letting her go. He hurt inside watching her struggling to walk. Why was she so sure it was Angel he wanted? He'd barely had a conversation with Angel. He didn't understand women at all.

THE PAIN of walking exhausted her but she wasn't about to stop. She half expected Dillon to catch up with her, but he didn't. She made it to the smithy and asked Homer to drive her home.

She had to bite her lip to keep from crying while he drove the wagon. She got down herself and hurried into the house. She'd return home shamed but she wasn't going to look like some poor beggar woman. Grabbing the lace Dillon had given her, she went into her bedroom, found her sewing supplies, and then took a dress out of her wardrobe.

Her jaw dropped. It had been shortened and the bodice was ridiculously low. The sewing was atrocious. She could fix it, but what had Elda been thinking? She propped her foot up on a pillow and examined the hem. The stupid woman had cut it instead of hemming it. The lace was much needed after all.

She threaded her needle and went to work. By the time she was done, the dress looked better than before. Normally she'd be overjoyed with her success, but she didn't feel like anything other than a colossal failure. She didn't plan to leave the family house once she finally got there. She laid her hand on her abdomen and frowned. There would be no babies for her. Dillon might go on with his life and remarry, but she wouldn't. It wouldn't be right.

All her past behavior had come back to haunt her. She was being punished for being mean. She'd have to accept it for it was, God's will. She'd made others unhappy, and it was all rushing back to her. There were always consequences but she never gave them much thought. Funny how she'd convinced herself this was her chance at happiness.

Would Dillon make arrangements for her to leave or would he make her stay and still build his other house? It would be the worst thing imaginable to have him and his strumpet living next door. The town's people probably wouldn't be shocked. They all liked Dillon. Done with the dress, she tried to stand. Hot pain sliced through her ankle, making her cry out. She'd have to get used to it. She was on her own, at least for a while if Dillon would let her go.

She hobbled to the window and realized that her view would be of his house. She hadn't explored upstairs yet. At first, she hadn't wanted to know how much more there was to clean, and then she'd hurt her leg. She'd move into Dillon's room as soon as she had the energy.

Settling herself back on the bed, she prayed and asked God to bring peace to her heart.

DILLON RAN his fingers through his hair as he stared down at his wife. Her eyes were red and swollen and her face was blotchy. What was he supposed to do now? He had never planned to ask Angel to move in with him. Had Scarlett's imagination run away with her? It didn't seem like she'd be willing to listen to him, though. She wasn't happy, and he couldn't make her happy. He'd have to let her go. He couldn't be the cause of her pain anymore. He refused to have a marriage full of fighting with spiteful words hurled about.

He went into the kitchen and poured cold water into a basin then grabbed a few towels and some clean bandages. She'd probably made her ankle worse, and he should have checked her leg that morning. He sighed. As soon as she was well, she'd leave him. That realization hurt more than he could have ever imagined.

He brought everything into the bedroom and set them down on the table next to her bed. She still slept. He lifted her skirt and took off her stocking. Just as he thought, her ankle was very swollen. In fact, it looked worse than the original injury.

After wetting a towel, he wrapped it around her ankle.

When he looked up he was met by her glare. At least she didn't try to pull away.

"You injured it again. I think it's worse than it was before. I wasn't very nice to you today and I'm sorry. You don't deserve my ire. You told me the truth, which I'm sure was hard to do, and I ended up angry at you. I put you in an, impossible situation, and I apologize."

He took the towel off and examined her ankle again. You'll need to stay off it completely. No wandering around Silver Falls with a walking stick. You could do permanent damage to yourself. You could end up lame."

She opened her mouth and then closed it. It looked as though she swallowed hard before she nodded. "It does hurt more than it did before."

"We'll keep it elevated and wrapped with cool towels. I'm hoping we can get the swelling to go down. I have to look at your leg now."

A grimace twisted her expression, and then she nodded.

He almost smiled when she gritted her teeth. He lifted her skirts up higher and gently put his hand on her thigh. She jumped but soon settled down, though her face turned bright red. It was nice to know she wasn't totally immune to him. What it would mean in the long run, he didn't know.

He checked her stitches and caressed the skin around them. The surprise on her face pleased him. He could be patient and kind.

He put her skirts to right and smiled at her. Then he climbed into bed with her, pulled her into his arms, and gently set her head on his shoulder. Her body was so stiff.

"You can go to your own room," she told him. "I think you being in here is causing my ankle to throb."

His lips twitched as he lay his cheek against the top of her head. There was a sense of rightness lying in bed with Scarlett in his arms. She smelled of roses and he promised himself he would plant some around the house. Perhaps that would make her happy. Her happiness was growing increasingly important to him. He wanted to laugh. She held herself straight as a fire poker.

"I think we can talk and be comfortable right here." He rubbed her arm. "First of all, there will not be another house."

"But I saw the plans!"

Kissing her on the top of her head kept her from pulling away. "I did draw those. I was mad and I was hurt. I drew them when I left to live at the smithy."

"I know you can't tolerate me very well." The sadness in her voice made his heart squeeze.

"I had hoped we'd get off to a better start. Most of the women in this town like me and my money. I'd hoped you'd like me for me, but the moment you insisted on servants, I knew you only liked my money. You certainly didn't seem to like *me*. I built dreams around our marriage from the moment Smitty told me about you." He sighed. "My parents were yellers who fought incessantly. There was never a moment of peace in the house, and I wanted us—you and me—to be different. But we started off with a huge fight, and I was willing to build my own separate house to gain the peace I craved."

"Did Angel have much input into the plans?" She stiffened and held her breath.

"No, of course not. There is nothing between Angel and me. I'm married to you."

Slowly she let her breath out. "She knows more about your bare body than is seemly. Please, Dillon, don't lie to me."

Having patience was harder than he'd thought it would be. "She's never even seen me without a shirt on. I don't know what game she's playing."

"I do. She wants you, and she plans to have you. She told

everyone she was going to live in the new house with you with the hope that I'd just leave town. It was then I realized I'd never have a child of my own. I couldn't just pretend we were never married and start over with another man. I meant my vows when I said them and to me they are sacred."

His heart squeezed again. Had she not heard him when he'd said the very same thing to her?

She sighed. "Besides Ma always has newborns at the house, and I thought they might act as a substitute. But my heart didn't quite agree with my idea." Her body relaxed against him. "Angel told these things to her friends. I don't understand what she had to gain by telling them lies."

"I don't either unless she wanted the gossip to get back to you. Those women aren't known for keeping secrets. Honey, I want children too. With you. I want us to try to make our marriage work. We can't rely on what others tell us."

"Perhaps, but I still want to go home. My heart hurts so much, and I don't think I'll ever be the same again. I swore when my parents died, before the Settlers adopted me, that I'd never love again. I'd never give anyone my heart because I knew the price of loss. I've given all that I have."

He shifted closer and stroked her back. She had so much more inside her. She was just afraid. Somehow, he'd have to reach her. "Do you find me pleasing to look at?"

She pushed up against his chest until she stared at him. Her brows furrowed, unfurrowed and then furrowed again. Crimson crept into her face. She then laid her head against his chest. "I suppose you're not unsightly."

A chuckle escaped. "I'm glad we have that cleared up. I find you to be beautiful, and when you're happy, you make my heart smile."

"You're just trying to be a charmer. I thought we were going to be honest."

"It's true. Can't you feel my heart beat faster?"

She nodded.

"That's because you're near. You make me feel excited."

She was quiet for a moment. "Do you mean that funny feeling you get in the pit of your stomach? I feel that too whenever I see you. It's a strange feeling, and I have no idea why it only happens with you."

"Although I'm just a bit better than unsightly, you're attracted to me in a way a women is attracted to a man she cares about."

"Ah, but what if you weren't my husband?"

"Then you ignore it and don't act on it. I know plenty of marriages where the couple is unhappy. I've known plenty that make the best of it and then there is a marriage like ours where we want to be with each other."

She tried to roll away from him. "If being with each other is what I think it is, I don't want any part of it. When traveling on a wagon train, I heard plenty. Men hit their wives and the cries of pain as they rutted will never leave me. I know it's my duty, but I think I'll pass."

He pulled her to him again trying to be as gentle as he could. "You plan to take a pass? Scarlett, there is so much passion bottled up inside you, I don't think you'd be able to pass for long. I have complete confidence we'll have those children we both want."

Her body became rigid again. "I don't think so. My mind is made up."

"I'd never hit you, or hurt you. It can be pleasant."

She laughed. "You tell a good tale."

He gently rolled her onto her back and then hovered over her. He lowered his weight a bit at a time taking care not to hurt her. Her lips were so rosy red, and he couldn't help but stare. He leaned down until their lips met. Hers were as soft as he imagined, and as he deepened the kiss she wrapped her arms around his neck. Apparently, she wasn't immune to his kisses.

The little sounds she made encouraged him to deepen the kiss, and he moaned. If he didn't stop soon, there would be no stopping. Regretfully, he eased his body off hers and shifted to lie at her side. Her expression of disappointment delighted him. They'd have those babies, he was sure of it now. He'd just have to use that patience God talked about.

CHAPTER NINE

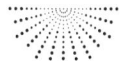

The next morning, Scarlett woke to the smell of coffee. The indentation in the pillow next to her was deep. Had Dillon stayed the night in her bed? Heat rushed into her face, but she was delighted. Would they really be able to move past all the hurt and love each other? Sometimes she felt as though she was half in love with him, but every time she felt that way something always came up to show her he didn't want her.

Maybe she needed to buck up and not care what the gossips in town had to say. Wasn't that what Dillon had told her last night? Perhaps it was time to believe in her husband. It was tempting, and the notion of it warmed her inside, yet she was still afraid. They were married for better or for worse and so far, until last night she'd seen mostly the worst.

Dillon walked in with a cup of coffee. "Here you go. I'm glad I didn't have to wake you."

She smiled and sat up. She took the steaming cup from him and smiled. "Where did you sleep last night?"

"In heaven." His eyes twinkled.

"What?"

"I slept with you in my arms, and it was heavenly. Did you know you have a slight snore?" He chuckled.

"I do not!"

"If you say so. It must have been that mangy cat."

She sipped her coffee and stole glances at him.

"I have two options for you today. You can either come to the smithy with me or I could find someone to come up here."

She didn't have to think about it. "I'll come with you. I hope it's not a repeat of yesterday." She frowned as she put the cup down on the bedside table.

Dillon sat on the edge of the bed. "I promise to be nice to you. I know I ignored you yesterday and I was wrong. I'd really like it if you came to work with me." He gave her a heart stopping grin.

"I'll need help dressing." Warmth filled her whole body.

"I'd be happy to help." He gave her a wink.

"No winking, no enjoying, got it?"

He laughed hard. "I can promise no winking but as for the no enjoying, I think that will be impossible."

She crossed her arms in front of her. "Oh, bother. I fixed the blue dress over there on the chair. I could wear that."

He went and picked it up. "Wow you must be good with a needle."

"Thank you. Yes, that and I have an eye for style. I've made lots of clothes for people. My pride got in my way once, and the preacher made me go and make dresses for my sister-in-law. She's nice and all, but she'd spent most of her life dressing like a boy. It was a challenge." It was nice to talk to him about her life. Maybe, just maybe, they could find common ground.

The whole time Dillon helped her to dress, she thought she'd die from embarrassment. He pretended he didn't see anything, but there was no help for it. At least he was a real gentleman. Things were so different between them. They laughed and joked, and she found she liked him as a person. He was the first real friend she'd ever had.

When they were ready to leave, Dillon went outside to hitch up the wagon. She clasped and unclasped her hands as her nerves began to fray. Yesterday had been bad, but it wasn't just because Dillon wasn't happy with her. Many people had contributed with their stares and whispers. Did she even have enough energy to hold her head up?

Dillon walked in, swung her up into his powerful arms, and held her close. She could feel the strength and hardness of his chest muscles. Somehow, he made her feel so very safe and liked. She stared up at his face trying to read him.

"What?"

"No one ever liked me before. I'm just having a hard time believing someone like you would want me around."

He set her up onto the wagon bench and frowned. "I will just have to prove to you that you are indeed likable. As long as you and I get along, I really don't care what anyone else has to say. There's just a shortage of eligible men around here is all."

"They all seem to think you're still eligible." Her mood plummeted.

He was silent as he drove until he pulled the lines to stop the horses and set the brake. Then he turned in his seat to face her. He kissed her on the mouth, and it wasn't just a quick kiss either. He whistled when he jumped down off the wagon and came around her side to get her.

"It'll be just fine." He held her close again as he carried her into the smithy. Homer's list looked exceedingly long. "It looks like it'll be a long day," he whispered to her.

He sat her down on the sofa and then picked her back up again. "Homer and Lou, could you two move the couch closer to where the others sit? I don't want my wife sitting by herself."

Her face grew hot, but she couldn't deny that the extra time in Dillon's arms was welcome. It made her feel good inside that he didn't want her sitting in the corner all alone. How it would work out, she didn't know.

After the sofa was moved, he set her down and fluffed the pillow behind her back. He arranged the blanket and handed her Ivanhoe. He only seemed to have eyes for her.

"Ahem!" Melly folded her arms in front of her and tapped her foot.

Dillon took his time turning around. "Was there something you needed? I'm going to be busy most of the day."

Melly smiled at Dillon and then she glared at Scarlett. "I made some cookies, and I wanted to know if I should bring some by."

Dillon shrugged. "I like cookies. Scarlett, are you partial to cookies?"

Scarlett's lips twitched. "It really depends on what kind they are."

"What kind are they, Melly? Sugar? Ginger snaps? Oatmeal?" Dillon asked.

Melly's jaw dropped for a moment. "You shouldn't ask. The polite thing to do is say 'yes, thank you, I'd love some cookies.'"

Dillon nodded. "Bring them and someone will want them. Thank you."

Melly looked as though she was gritting her teeth. She gave Scarlett another glare before she turned and left the shop.

Dillon winked at Scarlett and then asked to see the list Homer had put together. "We might as well start."

As nervous as she was, Scarlett expected to make a fool of herself or embarrass Dillon, but when the other men saw how attentive Dillon was to her, they fell in line. They included her in the conversation and seemed to value her opinion.

It was so different from having people crowd around her because they thought her the most fashionable or the prettiest. Her insides warmed, and she felt well regarded. People shuffled in and out all morning. It was a wonder that Dillon got as much work done as he did.

When she spotted Lolly crossing the street toward them, she wanted to groan. Dillon thought her to be a nice woman, but she had quite a glare. She might be outwardly sweet to him but she had an agenda.

Lolly smiled at Dillon but as soon as she saw Scarlett her smile disappeared. Scarlett kept a smile on her face. She didn't need to sink to Lolly's level.

Dillon took the basket from Lolly and thanked her. He didn't chat with her as he usually did. Instead, he put the basket on the shelf and fixed plates for both him and Scarlett.

She tried to make more room for him as he sat on the edge of the couch, but he handed her a plate and then put her legs on his lap. All eyes were on them, but she didn't care. Dillon gave a warm smile.

"Might as well eat while it's hot," Dillon said.

Lolly stood there, her face filled with outrage. After a last, long glare, she turned and left.

"I think you just lost an admirer." Scarlett said.

"She'll come around. She's known that I wasn't interested in a relationship with her."

Scarlett tilted her head. "Why?"

"Let's just say her husband was one of my best friends, and I know things I refuse to gossip about."

"I can respect that." She took another bite of meat pie. "She sure is a good cook."

"Ain't that the truth!" Lou said with his mouth full.

Scarlett pretended she didn't notice his lack of manners.

"Do you think Miss Melly will be bringing those cookies by soon?" he asked.

Homer laughed. "Don't be dense. She only wanted Dillon to have the cookies. She has no boundaries. She never has. She's still trying to win his favor." He shook his head.

Lou frowned. "Cookies would have been nice is all."

Dillon exchanged amused glances with her. "I guess we should get back to it." He waited until the other two men had moved away from them. "Do you need to use the privy?"

Her face warmed. "Not right yet, but thank you for asking."

Dillon put their plates back into the basket and set it on a shelf near the front. He walked back to Scarlett, fluffed her pillow again, and covered her with the blanket. Then he leaned down and kissed her cheek, before he returned to his work.

A warm glow filled her for the rest of the day. She couldn't keep her eyes off him. He was so strong and enticing. No man had ever had her attention the way Dillon did. They could be friends she decided but as far as anything else, she had to draw the line. He could kiss her and hold her but just as she already told him she'd rather not.

He'd adjust his expectations, she was sure of it. She'd learn to be a good friend and that should make him content. As soon as her ankle was healed, she'd cook and take care of the house. Not because he expected it, but because she wanted to.

His smiles were interfering with her reading. She almost laughed at her thoughts, but then Angel walked in and sidled up to Dillon.

"Will you be by again tonight, lover?" she purred. She put her hand on his chest as she batted her eyelashes at him.

Dillon showed no emotion. He just removed Angel's hand from his chest. "I have work to do."

"After work. Shall I expect you?" She glanced at Scarlett. "How about the usual time?"

Dillon laughed. "Honestly, I don't know what kind of game you're playing at, but I plan to go home with my wife. You remember my wife, don't you?"

"You didn't seem to mind—"

"Angel, give it up. I have never talked to you alone, and we most certainly did not... I take my marriage vows seriously, and I'm sorry as can be that I didn't make that clearer to you. I've done nothing to be ashamed of. I suppose my mistake was in allowing you to come and go as you pleased. Unless you have need of a blacksmith, I'd like it if you stayed away."

Angel's eyes grew wide. Then she turned to Scarlett. "This is your fault. You didn't want him and I did. What's so wrong with that?"

Dillon stood between Angel and Scarlett. "Please leave, Angel."

"Fine!" She whirled around and hurried away but not before she looked at Scarlett with vengeance in her eyes.

Scarlett was shocked. Dillon had gone way above what she expected. Happiness filled her. She finally had a friend. She watched him work. He was so very confident. His arms around her wouldn't be unwelcome. Perhaps when they got home.

As her face grew warmer thinking about Dillon, she pretended to read. She never was one to school her emotions. It got worse as the day went along. Each time she glanced up, he was staring at her. Did everyone else notice? Looking around, she realized they did and the men elbowed each other, smiling at her.

Fred Younger came in and announced that they found what had caused Matilda's rash. "Apparently, she was using poison ivy leaves in the privy. I guess no one told her those leaves weren't to be used."

"I'm just glad she's all right," Scarlett remarked without looking up from her book.

"Um, yes ma'am. I'm mighty glad too."

She wanted to meet this Matilda who was so popular with the men. It must be a horrid way to make a living, but sometimes a woman was left with few choices in life. She paused in the middle of turning a page. When had she started feeling bad for people less fortunate than her? She mulled it over. Dillon must have changed her in more ways than she'd thought.

Dillon still hadn't checked everything off his list, but he took off his leather apron and hung it on a peg. "Gentlemen, I'm taking my beautiful wife home. I don't want her overtired. Homer and Lou can handle things here for a bit."

Dillon took the blanket off of her. "Ready?"

She nodded as her skin tingled. She'd be in his arms again. There was no better place to be. "Yes, let's go home."

He lifted her into his arms and tucked her head under his chin. Then he boosted her onto the wagon bench. He got on and turned toward her. "Did you mean it when you called the house home?"

Shyly, she nodded.

Dillon framed her face with his calloused hands and then swooped down for a kiss. It started out as a gentle kiss of thanks, but it turned into something she didn't quite understand. The more he kissed her, the more she wanted to kiss him back. Her body felt as though it was on fire and though it was worrisome, she didn't pull away. After a while, she came up for air.

She was oddly breathless, and she wanted him to kiss her again, but when she glanced at him, he looked strange.

"Did I do something wrong?" She worried her bottom lip waiting for his answer.

Dillon caressed her cheek. "No, quite the opposite. I've never felt this way from a kiss before, and I like it." He unwrapped the reins from the brake, and they set out.

She placed both palms on her heated cheeks. "What did that mean?"

He chuckled. "I find your innocence enchanting. It's a good thing. I promise."

Nodding, she sat back. She wasn't sure if it *was* a good thing. He made her feel desire, and she wasn't ready for such a step. The kissing was very nice though.

DILLON STARED down at his sleeping wife. It had been four weeks since he'd moved the sofa closer to the visitors in the smithy. At first, he'd thought they'd just clear out and meet elsewhere but they hadn't. In fact, they all became fast friends with Scarlett. She was good at bantering with them. He could see an appreciation for her in their eyes.

She was a fun woman who had a sense of humor. It had almost been like meeting a completely different person. They touched each other whenever possible, and at first, he'd gotten some comments from his friends about them being newlyweds. In the evening, they sat on the front porch swing and talked about their day.

At night, he helped her undress and slip into her nightgown. It was growing harder to be patient. They slept in the same bed. She used his chest as a pillow, and he held her through the night. Then he'd help her dress the next day.

He prayed many times for the strength to wait for his wedding night, but it was getting to him. The frustration he'd been keeping inside was getting ready to blow. Soon, he hoped for soon. He'd have to talk to her about it. Her ankle was healed up and today was going to be her first day staying home. It would be lonely without her at the smithy.

Her eyes opened and she immediately smiled. "Good morning."

He leaned over and kissed her. She wrapped her arms around his neck and when he would have pulled away, she held on to him.

"Scarlett, a man can only take so much before he feels the need to be intimate with his wife."

"I'm ready. I've been waiting, but you've been so sweet." Her gaze met his and held.

"I didn't want to push you."

"I want us to be a properly wedded couple. Maybe a child will be the result."

Her face was aglow, and he couldn't wait any longer. He groaned and took her mouth, kissing her deeper. "As long as you're sure."

"I'm sure."

Dillon ended up being late for work that day, but he whistled as he worked.

CHAPTER TEN

Scarlett exercised her leg and ankle every chance she got. She finally went up to the second floor of the house and found a massive room with a huge bed, decorated for a king. Dillon must have intended for this to be their room. She frowned. If they slept in such a big bed would they lose the intimacy they had now in the small bed?

There were five other bedrooms, all unfurnished. She blushed. Dillon wanted to fill these rooms with children. Hopefully soon, but it was all in God's time.

The sound of the wagon caught her attention and she hurried to the front window in their bedroom. It was Dillon. Was something wrong? She took care going back down the stairs.

The door opened and Dillon smiled at her.

"How would my best girl like to go see a few waterfalls?"

"Really? I'd love to. What about work?"

He shrugged. "The list was unusually short today. Homer and Lou can handle it." He had his hands behind his back, and when he brought them in front of him, he had a pair of women's boots in his hands.

"Oh! Thank you!" She took the boots and hurried to a chair. She sat and shucked her shoes and then put on the new boots. "Perfect fit! Why are you smiling like that?"

"I guess I feel blessed to have found a wife that gets so excited to get boots for a gift."

"I agree, lucky you are! Let's go!"

They walked outside to the wagon, and Dillon helped her up. She missed him carrying her, but being healed was better. She smiled as they drove down the hill and straight through town. He turned and passed the first couple of falls, and he stopped at one that looked to be so tall it was as if the water was pouring from the sky.

"It's beautiful. Listen to the roar of the water. I swear I see colors of blue, green, and white in it." She hurried down from the wagon and got a bit closer. "Look! One falls goes into another. Double falls, how exciting."

"It's a bit narrower than the other falls. I like it because it seems calmer that the rest."

She nodded. "It's a bit romantic surrounded by the trees. Can we hike down to the bottom?"

"Not this time. When your ankle is much stronger we will. In fact we'll make it our mission to see all ten falls. This one is the tallest; at least it looks that way." He put his arms around her and pulled her close. "Not many people come to this one. Maybe we could stand under the falls next time."

"And get wet? You can. I'll watch."

He laughed. "I wasn't planning on wearing clothes, love."

Her eyes opened wide as her mouth formed an O.

"Before you get embarrassed, just think how romantic it could be. Just you and me and nature." He grinned. "I don't think I've ever seen you so red before."

"I'll let you know."

"As long as the answer is yes."

She laughed and turned to face him. She put her arms

around his neck and pulled his head down for a searing kiss. He seemed surprised at first, but soon enough he was deepening the kiss and rubbing her back.

"What? Aren't I allowed to initiate the kiss?"

His grin was sexy as he gazed at her. "Love, you can kiss me anytime."

Her face burned. She was a married woman but she couldn't help the fact that she seemed to be constantly blushing. She leaned her forehead against his chest hoping her face would return to its normal color.

"I like that you blush. I find it endearing." He kissed the top of her head. "We should probably get back since we have a big day tomorrow."

She lifted her head and stared into his eyes. "What's going on tomorrow?"

"Terry invited us over for lunch with his daughter Patty. He wants to get to know you better."

"He's been at the smithy plenty," she commented.

Dillon let go of her and chuckled. "He said he wanted to be able to talk without the subject of Matilda's rash being the center of attention."

She couldn't help but laugh. "Too bad they didn't know what it was from the beginning. I know of a salve I could have made for her. It'll be nice to get to know Patty too."

"Good. Oh, Patty wanted to know if you could wear one of your fancy dresses so she could see it. I happened to mention to Terry that you know how to sew wonderful creations, and now Patty can't wait to talk to you about dresses."

"Wonderful creations? Did you really say that?" Her lips twitched.

"No, I don't think so. It must have been words Patty used or something. Terry and I don't talk about pretty dresses that way or dresses in general. Let's get you home so you can rest up for tomorrow."

She nodded and smiled as he lifted her up onto the wagon. She cherished the closeness she now shared with him. To think she had almost left such a fine man. It would have been the biggest mistake of her life. She loved him so much it hurt. She'd been waiting for him to say he loved her before she said anything, but maybe she should say it first. She watched him drive, staring at his profile. What if he didn't say it back? He did say he wanted to be friends.

Turning her head, she watched the scenery. It would kill her if he didn't love her. Perhaps not knowing was better. She was glad when the house came into sight. She had a lot of thinking to do. She also needed a good night's rest. Her husband had been keeping her up at night, not that she minded in the least.

THE NEXT DAY, Dillon dressed in his Sunday best. It'd been hard to hide the surprise from Scarlett. It had been even harder to arrange everything. Thank goodness for Terry.

He stood at the bottom of the stairs. Now that her ankle had healed, they now shared the big bedroom on the second floor. "Are you about ready?" he called.

He didn't get an answer, but he didn't need one. She stood at the top of the stairs as pretty as a picture. Her red dress was stunning. She looked lovely. She'd left her hair down, and he couldn't help but stare.

Gracefully, she walked down the stairs, gazing into his eyes the whole time. He held out his hand and helped her down the last few steps.

"You are stunning. Patty is going to have a great time asking you questions."

She glowed at his praise. "I dressed for you. I want you to be proud to have me as your wife."

He would have hugged her but he was afraid he'd mess her hair. "I'm always proud to have you as my wife."

He led her out to a beautiful carriage.

"Oh, how pretty!"

"The owner wanted me to drive it. He says the wheel squeaks, but when I've driven it down the street in town I never hear it. Maybe I'll hear it this time," he lied.

He offered her his hand and helped her into the carriage. He rounded the other side and got in. "This is going to be fun. I've been looking forward to it. Terry has been such a good friend to me. We traveled to Oregon on the same wagon train. It's a shame his wife died on the trip. He has Patty though. She kept him going through his grief. He did well for himself and now he's being hounded by the single women."

"Oh, just like you were. I don't envy him that." She leaned back and smiled. "It sure is a fine carriage. I don't hear a squeak do you?"

"No I don't. I'll be able to report I drove it clear out to the Boxer ranch and didn't hear a thing."

"Are we almost there?"

"We certainly are." He drove the team up a hill and the ranch came into view.

"Who are all those people? I thought it was a small luncheon."

"It's a surprise for you. We never had our reception, and Terry offered to host it."

"That's sweet of him. My, there certainly are a lot of people there. It must be the whole town!"

"It certainly looks that way. Ready? Here's the turn off."

"I'm both excited and nervous. Don't leave me alone with any wicked women."

"I promise."

As they got closer, they could make out the faces of the people and Scarlett gasped.

"What on earth? Is that—?" Her mouth dropped open.

"Yes it is. Hold on, we're almost there."

"There's my ma and pa. Oh Dillon, thank you." She hugged him hard.

"Love, let go. I'm trying to drive." He waited until she was sitting down again. "Don't you know I just want you to be happy?"

She stared at him for a moment. "Of course I do, and I want you to be happy too."

"Let's skip the party and go home. I think we could find something exciting to do there."

She turned a becoming shade of red.

As soon as he stopped the carriage, she practically flew out of it straight into her ma's arms. Then she hugged her pa. After that, it was a long procession of brothers and sisters. She took Dillon's hand. "I want you to meet my family."

"This is Lynn, my ma and Smitty, my pa. Of course, you already know my pa. This is little Rose. Next is Greg, his wife Mercy and their daughter Hannah. This is Juan and his wife Sonia, their son Brent and their baby Zacharias. Zacharias means God remembered. This is Hunter holding Oscar's hand. Carlos, Anthony, Cynthia and in her arms is Alex. Jax, Will, Brian, Mia and this little girl she's holding is Christy. And this fine fellow is Cotten."

"I've heard so much about all of you I feel as though I know you all," Dillon greeted with a big smile. "Scarlett, we need to say hello to our hosts."

Scarlett nodded and readily took his offered hand. "We'll be back. I'm dying to hear what I've missed."

She gave his hand a gentle squeeze. "You've been keeping this a secret for a while haven't you?"

Dillon entwined his fingers with hers. "It wasn't easy. I knew it would make you happy and a couple times while you were recuperating I almost spilled the beans. I'm glad I didn't, your face is glowing with joy."

"Where have you been hiding them?"

"Terry has been taking care of them. They got in late yesterday, and they plan to leave in the morning."

"Such a short visit?"

"They have a ranch to run."

She nodded. "I understand, but I don't have to like it. Oh, there's Terry with his daughter Patty."

Dillon looked in the direction she indicated and smiled. "Let's go and thank him and enjoy our day. It's not every day we'll get a party thrown for us."

Terry shook Dillon's hand and gave Scarlett a huge hug. "A bigger turn out than I expected," Terry said.

"I wish I could say it's because we are popular but you know how nosey the people of this town are," Dillon said his voice full of humor.

"Everything looks so beautiful, Terry. I don't know how to thank you!"

"Scarlett, this is my daughter, Patty. She's been dying to meet you."

Scarlett smiled at the shy redhead. "I've wanted to meet you too, Patty," Scarlett greeted. "I hear you're interested in fashion. I'm glad to have finally found someone that shares my passion."

Patty's eyes glowed with happiness and Dillon was proud as could be of his wife. She wasn't the same spoiled little girl who had first arrived here. They'd had a few bad moments, but he had a feeling they'd have a long, fruitful, happy marriage.

The violins were tuning, and then the music began. He offered his arm to his wife. "Would you care to dance?"

She beamed at him and put her hand on his arm. "We've never danced before," her voice was delightfully shy.

Love filled his heart as he took her into his arms and they whirled around the dance floor. Gone was the haughty, scathing, insecure hellcat and it felt wonderful to have finally gotten down to the real Scarlett. The kind, giving, funny, caring wife that she'd become.

Their gazes met and locked. Her love for him was there for him to see. It was a promise of a lasting future. He doubted she'd ever want to go back to her parents again. Their nights together were magical and he wouldn't trade them for anything. To love and to be loved was such a gift, such a blessing. He hadn't known what he was missing all these years. He remembered his turning point.

Love is patient and kind; love does not envy or boast; it is not arrogant or rude. It does not insist on its own way; it is not irritable or resentful; it does not rejoice at wrongdoing, but rejoices with the truth. Love bears all things, believes all things, hopes all things, endures all things.

God's words had shown him the way, and if he hadn't listened, he'd have given up in defeat long ago.

"What are you thinking about?" Scarlett asked.

"I was thinking how lovely you are and how blessed we are to have such love between us."

Scarlett almost tripped but Dillon steadied her. "You love me?" There was hope mixed with fear in her blue eyes.

"Of course I love you. You're my heart. I'm happiest when I'm with you." He smiled.

Tears filled her eyes. "Oh Dillon, I've been waiting for you to tell me first. I was afraid to tell you. I'm not very loveable you know."

"You are loveable, Scarlett." She radiated happiness.

"Dillon, I love you too," her voice was soft as she said it. "We are so very blessed indeed." The music stopped and she took a step back. "I'd like to dance with my father. I know there are many women out there dying to dance with you."

He cocked his brow. "I didn't think you'd be happy if I danced with anyone else."

"I didn't either but I know our commitment is strong. Plus I can pull out the hair of any woman who tries to flirt with you."

He laughed. "I'd best keep an eye on you."

"That's always a good strategy. I don't even know what I'll do before I do it at times. You know most of the town is here and there are no people whispering about us or staring at us. It's nice."

"May I cut in?" Smitty asked. He hardly waited for a yes, before he drew Scarlett into his arms. He twirled her a few times and pulled her close. "Happy?"

'Yes, Pa, I am. More than I ever thought possible. You chose well for me. We had our problems at first and I wanted to go home, but Dillon wouldn't allow it. Did you know people want him to be mayor of the town but he's too busy? He also has the biggest house. At first I liked the house because it was the biggest, but now I like it because it'll hold all the children we plan to have."

Smitty smiled and kissed her on the forehead.

"I have to admit I thought you to be out of your mind having me marry such a tyrant. I've come to find that if you look at things with your heart, it's never what you thought. At least what I thought. I now wonder how you put up with me." She kissed his cheek.

"I've always known that you had a sweet, gentle, loving heart. I'd catch glimpses of it at times. It took a special love to bring it all out. Dillon is a good man. He too deserved love but he never seemed to think so. You look so happy, you glow. Of course we do miss you at the ranch, but knowing our little girl is happy makes it better."

"Little girl?"

"Oh, Scarlett you'll always be my little girl. I'll hold you in my heart, always."

"Pa, you're going to make me cry." She felt tears begin to form again.

Smitty took a step back and wiped the few tears that fell with the pads of his thumbs. "Be happy, you deserve it. Remember, we love you. We'd love if you could come and visit us."

She nodded. "That would be fun, wouldn't it? We'll have to see what Dillon's schedule is. He's the busiest man in town. Did you know he designs tools and houses? And that people come in to ask his advice about practically anything?"

"He's well respected. I bet you're an asset to him."

The music stopped, and her pa took her hand and led her to her ma.

Lynn pulled her in for a close embrace. "I've never seen you look so beautiful. You wear love well. He seems like a very nice man. Plus he's very nice looking. I worried about you but it looks as though I worried for nothing."

"Oh Ma, you had good reason to worry but we worked everything out. It was so bad he was going to build a separate house for himself right next door to me. I had a lot of growing up to do." Scarlett grimaced.

"My dear it happens to us all. It's hard to adjust to marriage at first but it seems as though you got through the hard part. The fact that he wanted us here proved to me that he holds your happiness as a high priority."

"Ma? I'm sorry I was such a trial to you."

Her ma laughed. "My dear, all children are a trial just in different ways. You need to embrace their uniqueness and try to gently guide them onto the right road. Now where did that husband of mine go? He promised me a dance."

They hugged again, and held on extra tight for a moment.

"Pa is over at the punch bowl."

Scarlett watched her ma hurry over to her pa. She spotted some of her siblings sitting under a tree with the little ones. She walked over and they all wanted to talk at once. It made her heart swell in a way it never had before when she lived at home. She sat and picked up Rose. It felt right to have a baby in her arms, and she wondered what her children would look like.

She felt the warmth of someone staring at her and she looked up. There stood Dillon with the oddest look on his face.

"Is something wrong?" she asked.

He sat on the ground next to her. "No, not at all. You look absolutely gorgeous with a baby in your arms. It suits you."

She felt her face heat under his gaze. "I never want this day to end. It's been so perfect, Dillon. I'm afraid I'll burst being so happy." She handed Rose to him.

For a moment he didn't seem to know what to do but it didn't take him long to figure out how to hold her. "She sure is cute."

Scarlett smiled. "You look good with a baby in your arms too." She laughed as his face reddened.

He handed the baby to Mia and stood, offering Scarlett his hand. "Let's dance. I never get enough of having you in my arms."

"Eww," a few of the younger siblings said.

Dillon just smiled as he walked to the dance floor with his wife on his arm. "Your family is very nice."

"Yes, they are. Thank you for arranging all this."

"I do believe you've thanked me a few times already." He took her into his embrace.

She never would stop loving the feel of his strong arms around her and his hard chest under her ear. There was nowhere better to be. The sun had gone down, and most of the food had been eaten. Unfortunately, the day was going to come to a quick end. It was a day she'd always remember.

It was hard to say goodbye but it was different this time. She knew she had Dillon and they had a good marriage. She hugged her pa last. He held her for a very long time.

"Don't you forget about us, now. I expect a visit when my grandchild is born."

"Oh, but I'm not…"

"You will be, my dear. All in good time." He squeezed her again. "I love you with my whole being. Always remember that. Now go to your husband. It does my heart good to see you both so happy." He kissed her cheek before he let her go.

Tears filled her eyes as she was drawn into Dillon's arms. "We should go," she whispered.

He nodded, and Hunter was right there with their carriage. As Dillon drove she looked back at her family for as long as she could. It wasn't very long in the dark. She'd miss them, but her home was here with Dillon. He was her heart and soul and her bliss.

"I bet Missy misses us. We're not usually gone at night."

Dillon laughed. "She's a cat, she can see in the dark. I'm sure she's fine."

"You're probably right. There are times I think she'd rather just be alone. I'd rather be with you."

He put both reins in one hand and entwined his fingers with hers. "That's good because you're stuck with me." He leaned over and kissed her. "I love you so very much, Scarlett.

"I love you too, Dillon.

EPILOGUE

Scarlett screamed so loud that Missy ran for cover. Dillon started to laugh, and she gave him the evil eye.

"This is all your fault and you laugh? When I'm done, I'm coming for you, Dillon Stahl! I think you need to feel some of this pain."

She sounded so serious that Dillon wiped the smile off his face. "I'm sorry." He took her hand, which she squeezed hard. "You have to admit it's not all my fault."

"Let's go to the double falls and have a romantic afternoon. Do you remember saying that to me? I do. You seduced me under the falls."

"I don't think husbands seduce, do they?"

"Now is a fine time to ask. Ohhh!!"

"You had fun that afternoon. You even wanted to go back and do it again sometime."

She squeezed his hand again. "I must have been out of my mind."

Dillon wiped her brow. Lolly was there to help, and she

told him that Scarlett was acting perfectly natural. "You'll be happy once the baby is born."

"And when will that be, Dillon? I've been in labor for days."

"It might seem that way, honey but it's only been a few hours."

"Don't honey me," she shouted as another contraction rippled through her body.

Dillon wisely kept his mouth shut.

She fell back against the pillow. "Do you think it will be a boy or a girl?"

He was almost afraid to answer. No matter what he said, it would be wrong. If this was what childbirth was like, he wondered why people stayed married. He had his choice to wait outside but he wanted to be there for her. Someone should have warned him. "A girl just like you."

"But what if it's a boy? You won't want it?"

Now he knew she was out of her mind.

"It won't be long now," Lolly said. The merriment in her eyes must be at his expense.

"Did you hear that? It won't be long. Remember how we cuddled last night? That was nice wasn't it?"

From the look on her face, he knew he'd somehow said the wrong thing again. He needed some whiskey. She squeezed his hand so hard he thought she'd break a few fingers. Then she stopped.

"Oh, she's beautiful," Lolly exclaimed. "Let me clean her up a bit."

"A daughter, Scarlett!"

Scarlett smiled. "I bet she'll be as sweet as me."

It was hard, but he kept a straight face. Sweet like her? Well Scarlett was sweet when she wasn't inhabited by the devil. He couldn't help it, he chuckled.

Scarlett glanced at him but didn't say a word. She held

her hands out and smiled when Lolly placed the baby in her arms.

"Look Dillon, she's beautiful! Hello Sylvia, welcome." Scarlett laughed at the look of surprise on his face.

"You want to name her after my grandmother?"

"You loved her, didn't you?"

His eyes misted. "Yes I did, and Sylvia is a beautiful name. Look at her hair it's so blond. She'll fit in. It's almost silver, you know like Silver Falls. Especially the double falls."

"If I didn't have Sylvia here in my arms I'd hit you," she smiled at him as she said it.

"I think we should call her Silver. It's a lovely name and it will always remind us of that lovely afternoon."

"Sylvia is her name." Scarlett shook her head and laughed. "What should I do with you?"

"She's going to have the best life ever. Maybe I should buy her a pony," he said enthused.

"Let's wait on the pony for a few years. I'm sorry I was so awful to you. If you must know I did enjoy the double falls after you proved to me that no one could see us behind the falls." She sounded more like herself and he was relieved.

"You still blush and it's very becoming. Have I told you that you are my world? You and Sylvia, and I love you both? I love you more than I ever thought possible. You're right; Silver will have the best life." He gave her his best grin. It really didn't matter what they call their precious baby girl. He closed his eyes and thanked God for Sylvia and he also thanked Him that both his girls were well.

THE END

I'm so pleased you chose to read Scarlett, and it's my sincere hope that you enjoyed the story. I would appreciate if you'd consider posting a review. This can help an author tremendously in obtaining a readership. My many thanks. ~ Kathleen

ABOUT THE AUTHOR

Sexy Cowboys and the Women Who Love Them...
Finalist in the 2012 and 2015 RONE Awards.
Top Pick, Five Star Series from the Romance Review.
Kathleen Ball writes contemporary and historical western romance with great emotion and
memorable characters. Her books are award winners and have appeared on best sellers lists including: Amazon's Best Seller's List, All Romance Ebooks, Bookstrand, Desert Breeze Publishing and Secret Cravings Publishing Best Sellers list. She is the recipient of eight Editor's Choice Awards, and The Readers' Choice Award for Ryelee's Cowboy.
Winner of the Lear diamond award Best Historical Novel- Cinders' Bride
There's something about a cowboy

- facebook.com/kathleenballwesternromance
- twitter.com/kballauthor
- instagram.com/author_kathleenball

OTHER BOOKS BY KATHLEEN

Lasso Spring's Series
Callie's Heart
Lone Star Joy
Stetson's Storm

Dawson Ranch Series
Texas Haven
Ryelee's Cowboy

Cowboy Season Series
Summer's Desire
Autumn's Hope
Winter's Embrace
Spring's Delight

Mail Order Brides of Texas
Cinders' Bride
Keegan's Bride
Shane's Bride
Tramp's Bride
Poor Boy's Christmas

Oregon Trail Dreamin'

We've Only Just Begun

A Lifetime to Share

A Love Worth Searching For

So Many Roads to Choose

The Settlers

Greg

Juan

Scarlett

The Greatest Gift

Love So Deep

Luke's Fate

Whispered Love

Love Before Midnight

I'm Forever Yours

Finn's Fortune

Made in the USA
San Bernardino, CA
02 January 2019